Chapter One

'Midnight,' said Grandwitch Sourmuddle. 'Time to begin. Everyone here, I take it?'

Twelve Witches and their Familiars sat at Witchway Hall's long table with an air of eager anticipation. This wasn't the usual monthly Coven Meeting.

That morning, everyone had risen to find a note on the mat. It read:

**IMPORTANT ANNOUNCEMENT.
WITCHWAY HALL, MIDNIGHT.
BE THERE.
SOURMUDDLE**

Important Announcements didn't happen often, and all the Witches had made an effort to be on time. Well, all except one.

'Pongwiffy isn't,' piped up Witch Sludgegooey in a telltale way. 'She knows about it, though. We saw her reading your note, didn't we, Filth? Before she threw it away.'

The small Fiend next to her nodded. 'For real.'

Sourmuddle sighed and raised an eyebrow at

Witch Sharkadder, who was Pongwiffy's best friend. Sometimes.

'Don't ask me,' said Sharkadder. 'Dudley and I haven't seen her for days. Not since she ate the frogspawn fritters I was saving.'

Dead Eye Dudley was Sharkadder's Cat. He didn't have much time for Pongwiffy. In particular, he had it in for Hugo, her Hamster Familiar. He made a disgusting noise somewhere between a spit and a snarl.

'*Yaaaarlllsssppitt!*'

Sharkadder wiped her eye and said, '*Careful,* Dudley. You splattered Mummy.'

'We'll start without her,' said Sourmuddle. 'I'm not waiting for her to drift in when she feels like it, trotting out the usual claptrap about losing a shoe or coming over all funny or stopping to put out a fire –'

She broke off at the sound of slamming doors, followed by hasty footsteps.

'Sorry I'm late!' called a breathless voice. 'Lost a shoe, took ages to find it because I came over all funny and then Hugo accidentally set fire to . . .'

'Enough!' snapped Sourmuddle. 'Not. Another. Word. You've got the green spots – I know you're lying. *Sit!*'

Everyone smirked as Pongwiffy sat. She was plastered in the inconvenient green spots that

2

always appear when she tells fibs. Hugo sat on her shoulder giving jaunty little waves to his fellow Familiars, who either waved back or blanked him, depending on their mood.

'Right. Time for the Announcement,' said Sourmuddle. 'Snoop? First Visual Aid, if you please.'

The small red Demon at her elbow ducked under the table, reappearing with a battered suitcase.

'What's that?' asked Witch Ratsnappy, frowning.

'It's called A Suitcase,' explained Sourmuddle. 'A handy receptacle used to transport things from one place to another.'

'I know *that*. But what's *in* it?'

'My things.'

'And why are they in a suitcase?'

'Because I'm going away.'

There was a united gasp. Sourmuddle going away? Just like *that*? This was new. This was worrying.

'It's all arranged,' said Sourmuddle. 'I'm off to visit my sister Chilliwaddle. She's just retired to the frozen north. Got herself a nice little cabin up in the Snowy Mountains. We're going to go dooboggling.'

'Tobogganing,' corrected Snoop.

'Yes. And raise mice.'

'Moose,' said Snoop. 'You're going to race moose.'

'I know. And she's going to teach me to . . . what was it again?'

'Skate on thin ice.'

'That's it. For which I will need a pair of wachamacallums.'

'Skates,' provided Snoop. 'Second Visual Aid?'

'If you please.'

Snoop scrabbled under the table and produced a pair of rusty ice skates.

'That's them,' said Sourmuddle. 'Snoop found them in Pongwiffy's Dump.'

Pongwiffy opened her mouth to protest, remembered she wasn't allowed to speak and shut it again. Most people had the manners to ask before removing things from her Dump, but Sourmuddle was Grandwitch and did as she liked. Including, it seemed, go off on holiday. Just like that.

'Aren't you a bit old for winter sports?' asked Witch Scrofula.

'Nonsense,' said Sourmuddle. 'You're never too old to learn new skills.'

'But what about Coven Meetings?' wailed Witch Bendyshanks. 'Who'll make decisions and tell us what to *do*? You know we never agree on anything.'

'Aye,' thundered Witch Macabre. 'Somebody has tae keep order. Ye need to appoint a Deputy, Sourmuddle. Somebody tough. That'll be me.'

'Why you?' howled Sludgegooey, to much

and the
Important
Announcement

Kaye Umansky

Illustrated by Nick Price

BLOOMSBURY

LONDON BERLIN NEW YORK

This book has been specially written and published for World Book Day 2010. World Book Day is a worldwide celebration of books and reading, with events held last year in countries as far apart as Afghanistan and Australia, Nigeria and Uruguay. For further information please see www.worldbookday.com

World Book Day in the UK and Ireland is made possible by generous sponsorship from National Book Tokens, participating publishers, authors, illustrators and booksellers. Booksellers who accept the £1 World Book Day Token kindly agree to bear the full cost of redeeming it.

Bloomsbury Publishing, London, Berlin and New York

First published in Great Britain in March 2010 by Bloomsbury Publishing Plc
36 Soho Square, London, W1D 3QY

Text copyright © Kaye Umansky 2010
Illustrations copyright © Nick Price 2009

The moral rights of the author and illustrator have been asserted

All rights reserved
No part of this publication may be reproduced or
transmitted by any means, electronic, mechanical, photocopying
or otherwise, without the prior permission of the publisher

A CIP catalogue record of this book is available from the British Library

ISBN 978 0 9562 8775 5

All papers used by Bloomsbury Publishing are natural, recyclable products made
from wood grown in well-managed forests. The manufacturing processes conform
to the environmental regulations of the country of origin

Typeset by Dorchester Typesetting Group Ltd
Printed in Great Britain by CPI Bookmarque, Croydon

1 3 5 7 9 10 8 6 4 2

www.bloomsbury.com
www.kayeumansky.com

support. Macabre was known to be heavy-handed. 'You're too bossy to be Deputy.'

Twin Witches Agglebag and Bagaggle nudged each other. Their Familiars (two identical Siamese Cats called IdentiKit and CopiCat) sat up hopefully.

'There's two of us,' said Agglebag. 'We'd be a *double-strength* Deputy, wouldn't we, Bag?'

'We would, Ag,' agreed Bagaggle.

'Nonsense!' chipped in Greymatter, who wrote poetry and considered herself the brains of the Coven. 'I'm clearly the obvious choice, and Speks agrees, don't you, Speks?'

The Owl sitting on the rafter nodded wisely, as Owls do.

'But I've got the looks!' That was Sharkadder, scrabbling in her bag for lipstick. 'Right, Duddles?'

'Arrr,' growled Dudley, who talked in a piratical way when he wasn't spitting in people's eyes.

'Why not me? Barry and I never get a look-in.'

That was Scrofula, sounding whiny. The bald Vulture on the back of her chair nodded dolefully and said, 'True. It *is* our turn to shine.'

There were some unkind titters. Scrofula suffered from chronic dandruff and Barry was always moulting. Shining was something they didn't do.

'Nonsense!' yelled Bendyshanks. 'It should be me!'

'No, me!'

'Meeeeee!'

Pandemonium broke out. It seemed that every Witch thought she would make a fine Deputy and was determined to shout the loudest. Well, all except Bonidle (asleep), Gaga (lost interest and dancing in a corner) and Pongwiffy (forbidden to speak).

Sourmuddle rapped for silence. Everyone simmered down and sat up straight, trying to look Perfect-Deputy-like.

'I knew it would be like this,' said Sourmuddle. 'That's why I contacted the Supreme Board of Grandwitches and they're sending over a – what's it, Snoop?'

'Supply.'

'Right. She's flying in tomorrow.'

Dead silence.

'Don't look at me like that,' said Sourmuddle. 'She'll be moving into my cottage to water the flowers and exercise Stumpy. No use for Broomsticks in the frozen north, Chilliwaddle says. They go bonkers trying to sweep up all the snow.'

'What's her name?' growled Macabre. 'This *Ootsider*?'

'Crackwippy,' said Sourmuddle. 'Grandwitch Crackwippy. Never met her myself, but she's probably charming. She wants you all here tomorrow night, midnight, on the dot. Hear that, Pongwiffy?'

Pongwiffy gulped and said nothing. Vernon (Ratsnappy's Rat) raised a paw.

'Permission to speak?'

'Make it quick,' said Sourmuddle. Familiars weren't encouraged to speak at Witch Meetings.

'Has she got a Familiar?'

All the Familiars held their breath.

'She has,' said Sourmuddle. 'A Crow. Called – what is it, Snoop?'

'Christine,' said Snoop.

There was a lot of aghast eye-rolling at this. As it happens, the Familiars are all male. No reason. They just are. And now there was the threat of a Crow called Christine. Ooo-er.

'Right, we're off.' Sourmuddle picked up her suit-case. 'I'll send a postcard.'

'Wait a minute!' shouted Sludgegooey. 'How long will you be gone? When are you coming back?'

'Depends how much I'm enjoying myself. I *might* like it so much I'll stay indefinitely. Just don't let me down in front of the Supply. She'll be sending a full report, so do as you're told.'

And with that, Sourmuddle and Snoop vanished. No flash. No smoke. No waiting for a bus or messing about with train timetables. One moment there, the next, *pfff*! Gone. That's how Grandwitches do it.

Just like that.

Chapter
Two

On the borders of Witchway Wood is a wet, windblown, damp-and-drippy cave area known as Goblin Territory. The Goblins who live there would love to move, but can't. Why they are stuck there is a long story which we won't go into now.

There are seven of them. One whole Gaggle. (There are always seven Goblins in a Gaggle, and yet Goblins can't count beyond two. Weird.) Their names are Plugugly, Stinkwart, Hog, Lardo, Slopbucket, Eyesore and Sproggit, and right now they are trying to sleep.

Outside, the full moon is sailing in the sky, filling the world with beautiful silver light. Inside, the Goblins are piled in an untidy heap, filling the cave with shouting. They are all wearing boots and bobble hats, apart from the Goblin at the bottom, who has a saucepan on his head.

Getting comfy in a cave is difficult.

'Ow! Get off, Stinkwart, yer elbow's in me eye!'

'Well, get yer knee out me ear, then!'

'Whose nose is this? Me finger's wedged up a nose and *it ain't mine*!'

'Stop *wigglin'*, Slopbucket! You're wigglin' all over

me like a – like a *wiggly* fing!'

'You callin' me a wiggly worm?'

'No, I'm callin' you a wiggly *fing*! Don't put worms in me mouf!'

'I'll put my *fist* in if you don't stop goin' on . . .'

There was a slithering sound followed by a series of bumps and pained cries as the Goblin at the bottom sat up.

'Ouch! *Now* see what you done! I bashed me 'ead!'

'Lie back down, Plugugly. You're the mattress – you ain't supposed to *move*!'

But Plugugly didn't lie down. Instead, he rose to his feet, spilling Goblins everywhere, straightened his saucepan and said crossly, '*Anudder* terrible night! Dis is *stupid*!'

'What is?' asked Hog, rubbing his head stupidly.

'Dis *bedtime* fing. All dis shoutin' an kickin'. An' me at de bottom gettin' de worst of it. It's not fair. 'Specially now I's used to finer fings.'

'What you on about? What finer fings?' sneered Lardo.

'Finer fings like sleepin' in a Proper Bed. When I was at de Giants' 'ouse dat time. When I was bein' Nanny Susan an' lookin' after Baby Philpot.'

This little speech refers to a past occasion when Plugugly disguised himself as a nanny and worked for the Stonkings, two Giants who had moved into

9

the area together with their Giant baby. He had indeed been given a bed of his own. It had been a glorious thing. But that is another long story we won't concern ourselves with now.

'Well, we ain't got a bed,' said Slopbucket. 'We just got floor.'

'Well, we *should* 'ave,' said Plugugly. 'A bed keeps you *off* de floor, so you can't feel de sharp little stones.'

'We don't feel 'em,' pointed out Eyesore. 'That's 'cos you're at the bottom, bein' the mattress.'

'That's what I'm *sayin*'. It's not fair.'

'Worse in the middle,' argued Lardo. 'No air.'

'Coldest on top, though,' chipped in Sproggit. 'An' further to fall when someone kicks. Like *you* do, Slopbucket.'

'So?' said Slopbucket. 'You snore.'

'So do you.'

'So do you.'

'So do –'

'You know what?' interrupted Plugugly. 'I's had enuff. I fink we should get a bed. Den we can 'ave a *good* night an' wake up feelin' nice for once.'

'Oh yeah?' jeered Eyesore. 'Where we gonna get a *bed* from?'

'I dunno yet,' admitted Plugugly. 'I's finkin'.'

'Reckon that ole Pongwiffy's got one on 'er Dump?' pondered Hog.

'No,' said Plugugly firmly. 'I doesn't want a dirty ole bed from a Witch's Dump. I wants a new one. Wiv bouncy springs an' a fick mattress an' white sheets an' fluffy pillers. An' a posh bedspread.'

'Bed spread?' Slopbucket looked puzzled. 'Does it come outta jars?'

''Course not!' scoffed Plugugly. 'A bedspread's the cover wot goes on top. It's got a coloured pattern.'

'Not flowers, I 'ope,' said Hog, alarmed. 'Flowers is sissy.'

'Yeah,' agreed Sproggit. 'Better to 'ave a Goblin Rangers pattern.'

This proved popular. The Gaggle were strong supporters of the Rangers, who were top of the Goblin Football League. Their kit was mud brown and sludge green.

'Yay!' yelled the Goblins, punching the air enthusiastically. 'Goblin Rangers! Yay!'

'It'd 'ave to be big, wouldn't it?' mused Hog. ''Ow'd we get it in the cave?'

At this, the enthusiasm waned a bit. How *would* they get a thumping great bed through the tiny cave entrance?

'It'd take up lotsa room,' said Lardo doubtfully. 'Where'd our stuff go?'

The enthusiasm waned a bit more.

'And 'ow we gonna pay for it?' asked Eyesore.

The enthusiasm fizzled out altogether. It always

came down to money – something the Gaggle never had.

'Back to the floor then,' sighed Stinkwart. 'Lie down, Plug.'

But Plugugly didn't want to lie down.

'No,' he said. 'I's not givin' up dat easily. I's goin' out for a walk to fink. Who's comin'?'

But an argument was breaking out about who should be the mattress and it looked like a fight was brewing. Clearly, nobody was coming with him.

So he went on his own.

Plugugly rolled back the boulder and stepped out into the moonlit night. Behind him came raised voices and the sound of Lardo's fist connecting with Hog's eye.

He sighed and set off down the hill, thinking about beds. He was halfway down the slope when a small shape detached itself from the shadows of a stunted tree and stepped into his path. It was the Thing in a Moonmad T-shirt. It had a sack over its shoulder and was holding a stack of cards in its hairy hand.

'I hope you're not going down into the Wood,' said the Thing. 'You know Goblins aren't allowed.'

'None o' your business where I's goin',' said Plugugly.

'I'm just saying. The Witches are having a

meeting. They'll be out soon. They'll zap you if they see you.'

'I know dat. I's just goin' down de hill an' up again.'

'What, to fetch a pail of water?' sneered the Thing.

'No, to kick you up de bum,' said Plugugly crossly.

'Talk like that and I won't give you one of these,' said the Thing, holding out a card.

Plugugly took it and stared down helplessly.

'Wot's it say?'

'You've got it upside down, stupid.' The Thing snatched the card and turned it the right way up. 'It's an advertisement, see. A new shop. *Helpful Bob's Essential Necessities Emporium*. It's got a lot of good deals.'

'It's got a lot o' long words. Wot's it sell?'

'Everything,' said the Thing. 'Everything you need. Cauldrons—wardrobes—prams—cuckoo clocks—telescopes—soap dishes—clarinets—lampshades—ugly vases—cameras—forks—accordions—wheelbarrows . . .'

'All right, dat'll do.'

'Coat racks—ironing boards—tin baths—pianos . . .'

'I said dat'll *do*.'

'Banana plantations—plastic scissors—useful screws—islands in the sun . . .'

'Stop! I's heard enuff!'

'I'm just saying. Bob sells everything. Got a warehouse full of stuff. If it's not in stock, he'll order it. Same day delivery. And you don't even pay.'

'Eh?'

'Special opening offer. Buy now, pay later.'

Plugugly stared down at the card. He said, 'Where is it?'

'There's a map on the back.'

'Wot's a map?'

'Oh, never mind,' sighed the Thing. 'Down the hill, turn left. Take the road north to Crag Hill. There's a big sign halfway up. *Helpful Bob's Essential Necessities Emporium*. You can't miss it. Well, *you* could, but anybody else couldn't.'

'Dat's all you know,' said Plugugly. And he thrust the card in his pocket and went hurrying back up the hill.

'I don't like the sound of her,' said Pongwiffy to Sharkadder, as they walked home through the moonlit Wood.

The Supply Grandwitch crisis had brought them together, and they were friends again. Even Dudley and Hugo had called a temporary truce.

'Sinister name, isn't it?' agreed Sharkadder, with a little shiver. '*Crackwippy*. Brr.'

'Whatever she's called, she's not telling me what to do,' said Pongwiffy. 'I'm not being bossed around by some pushy stranger. Neither will the others. There'll be trouble, mark my words.'

Behind them, Dudley and Hugo had started up a rare conversation.

'A *Crow*,' growled Dudley.

'A *girl*,' groaned Hugo.

'Blowed if I'm takin' no lip from no girl Crow.'

'Nor me. No vay. Zere gonna be trouble.'

Everybody stopped. They had come to where the path divided. One way lay Sharkadder's trim cottage, and the other way was Number One, Dump Edge, Pongwiffy's appalling hovel.

'Can I come in for a cuppa?' asked Pongwiffy hopefully.

'Not tonight, Pong, if you don't mind,' said Sharkadder. 'I'm feeling a bit emotional. It's just hit me. Sourmuddle going away and leaving us like that.'

'We'll miss her,' agreed Pongwiffy. 'She's got her irritating side, but we're going to miss her.'

They both heaved a sigh. Sourmuddle could indeed be annoying, but at least they knew her little ways.

'Suppose she never comes back?' snivelled Sharkadder. 'Suppose we're stuck with a Supply for ever?'

'We won't be,' promised Pongwiffy. 'Not if I've got anything to do with it.'

Behind them, Hugo and Dudley continued to

mutter in an undertone.

'Us'll mutiny,' said Dudley. 'Us b'aint 'avin' no *girl* joinin' the crew.'

'Right!' agreed Hugo. 'Ve show 'er all right. *Christine*. Huh!'

It was the first time they had ever agreed.

'I'll call for you tomorrow night, then,' said Pongwiffy.

'You do that,' sniffed Sharkadder. 'Come on, Duddles.' And they walked off.

The path leading to the hovel glowed quite clearly in the moonlight. That's why Hugo spotted the pile of cards that lay scattered beside the trail. The Thing in the Moonmad T-shirt had obviously got fed up and gone home.

'Vot zis?' said Hugo, picking one up. 'Look like advertisement.'

Pongwiffy plucked it from his paw.

'*Helpful Bob's Essential Necessities Emporium*,' she read. '*Special Opening Offers*.'

'Sound like new shop. Ve go look?' said Hugo.

Witchway Wood doesn't boast much in the way of shops. It's a dodgy place for the retail trade. There are a lot of shady types around who think nothing of breaking in and robbing (or possibly eating) the till. Pongwiffy was tempted. Then again . . .

'No,' she decided. 'Not tonight. I want to go

home and put my thinking cap on. We've got to come up with a Plan Of Resistance.'

'OK,' agreed Hugo. A Plan Of Resistance sounded a good idea. Whenever he thought about Christine, he broke out in a cold sweat.

Meanwhile, back in the Goblins' cave . . .

'Shop?' moaned Hog, clutching a black eye. 'What you on about – new shop?'

'Like I said!' shouted Plugugly, waving the card around. 'Dere's a shop opened. Some Bob geezer. It's more 'n a shop, it's a *Hempororium*! Wiv – Hessessenshul Nessessessessiteez.'

'Hessessenshul what?' asked Lardo. Plugugly took a deep breath.

'Ness-ess-ess-ess-ess-ess . . .' Sproggit banged him on the saucepan with a stick. '. . . ess-ess-(DOINGGG!)-*essiteez*! Ouch! Phew. I were stuck on dat word. Easy to start sayin' but 'ard to stop.'

'Wot are they?' Slopbucket wanted to know. 'Can you eat 'em?'

'No,' said Plugugly doubtfully. 'I don't fink so. Ir's more like – oh, I dunno. I can't remember now. Hard enuff rememberin' dat word.'

'What word?'

'Ness-ess-ess-ess . . .'

'Somebody dong 'im,' advised Eyesore, and Sproggit vigorously obliged.

17

DOINGGG!

'*Ouch!* All right, Sproggit, dat's enuff! I ain't sayin' no more. Tellin' you interestin' stuff an' gettin' whacked all de time.'

'Good,' said Slopbucket. 'We're tryin' to get some sleep 'ere. Lie down like a good mattress.'

'I will, I will! But before I forget, dere's just one fing . . .'

'Lie down!'

'But . . .'

'*Lie down!*'

So Plugugly lay down and everyone piled on top. Sharp little stones dug into his back. Elbows jabbed and boots kicked. All the breath was forced out of his lungs. It was ages before everyone finally settled down and began snoring.

Eventually, weariness overwhelmed discomfort, and Plugugly dozed off, quite forgetting what he had been about to say.

At first light, as the moon faded and the rising sun took over, he woke up with a start. It had come back to him!

He sat up. Slitherings, bumps and cries resounded as the shout rang around the cave.

'A BED! DAT'S IT! WE CAN BUY A BED!'

Chapter
Three

Witchway Wood is home to a great many species besides Witches. Skeletons, Trolls, Ghouls, Zombies, Vampires, Werewolves, Mummies, the occasional superstar – it would take too long to name them all. They don't mix much, but that doesn't stop gossip spreading.

By the time the sun had risen, the news was out. Grandwitch Sourmuddle had gone away! A Supply was taking over! Everyone was keen to see what the Witches would do.

But to everyone's disappointment, the Witches did nothing. All day they remained cooped up in their various caves and cottages. Front boulders stayed firmly in place. Curtains were kept drawn. Clearly, they were in a state of shock. Either that, or sulking.

At sunset, still no sign. Twilight darkened into night. Still no movement. Only as midnight neared did doors creak open and boulders roll back. Twelve figures emerged and set off in the direction of Witchway Hall.

Pongwiffy called for Sharkadder, as arranged. Sharkadder was wearing her best purple gown and

19

high-heeled shoes with purple bows.

'You're all dressed up,' sneered Pongwiffy from the doorstep.

'Not especially,' said Sharkadder.

'Yes, you are. You're all dressed up for the Supply.'

'I am *not*. Come on, we'll be late.' Sharkadder teetered down the path, moonlight gleaming off her long, sharp, heavily powdered nose.

'Well, *I'm* not making an effort,' said Pongwiffy, falling in step. 'I couldn't care less what she thinks.'

'Hear! Hear!' chimed two voices in unison. The twins were walking up the path with IdentiKit and CopiCat twining around their ankles.

'We've decided we're not taking orders from some outsider, haven't we, Bag?' added Agglebag.

'Quite right, Ag. She's not telling *us* what to do.'

'Good for you, twins. You tell her,' agreed Pongwiffy. 'I'll back you up.'

There came the sound of clattering hooves and Macabre burst from the trees, mounted on Rory, her Haggis.

'Right!' she snarled, hauling on the reins. 'Let's get this over with. Ah don't know what this *Crackwippy* character's like, but she'd better noo mess wi' *me*!'

More Witches and Familiars joined them as they made their way through the Wood. All talk was of rebellion. Pongwiffy explained her Plan of Resistance, which basically consisted of refusing to take orders.

'Suppose she *makes* us, though?' asked Scrofula. 'Grandwitches do what they like.'

'Then we'll do it really slowly. And sigh a lot. That'll wear her down, and then we'll explain how things are run round here. Agreed?'

'Agreed!'

By the time they reached Witchway Hall, their blood was up. The Familiars had also formed a united front – although it was a nervous sort of front. They were about to meet Christine. Oo-er!

The Hall lies in a glade in the middle of Witchway Wood. It is a cross between a large hut and a small theatre. The Witches use it for their monthly Meetings on chilly nights when they can't be bothered to fly to Crag Hill.

The chatter died away as everyone came to a halt.

'No sign,' said Pongwiffy. 'All quiet. D'you think she's in there?'

'Well, we'll soon find oot,' said Macabre. 'We'll just march in and . . .'

BOOOOOOOOOOOOOOOOOM!

Everyone jumped as a clap of thunder rent the air, accompanied by an eye-searing flash of lightning! The doors of the Hall burst open with an almighty crash!

Sickly green light streamed from the interior. Slithering Steve (Bendyshanks's Snake) fled into the folds of his mistress's cardigan. Rory reared, almost unseating Macabre. Filth the Fiend shouted, 'Time to split, dudes!' and dived behind a bush. Dudley backed between Sharkadder's legs, hissing. Even Hugo ducked behind Pongwiffy's hat.

And then – from out of the dazzling green light – there fell a horrible shadow. A long, thin shadow. It sort of . . . *oozed* across the glade. The source stood smack in the middle of the doorway.

A new Broom. Ludicrously tall. Toughened bristles fixed to an evil-looking stick. Twiggy arms folded like a bouncer's.

'Good grief!' gasped Greymatter. 'Is that *pure* Broom, or some sort of lamp post cross? I've never seen anything like it!'

'Now what?' gulped Scrofula. 'Do we go in?'

'Aye,' said Macabre, giving Rory a thump to calm him down. 'Come on, girls. Follow me.'

Uncertainly, keeping well clear of the Broom, everyone trooped forward into the blinding green glare. The doors slammed behind them.

Once inside, they assembled at the top of the central aisle. The new Broom stationed itself before the doors. No escaping now.

The seats facing the stage were empty. But the stage wasn't. Slap bang in the centre, lit by a harsh green spotlight that came from nowhere, was — a *throne*. A huge black carved throne with lion's feet and thick armrests.

Hunched on the throne, leering down through a mouthful of jagged teeth, was the Supply!

She was all in black, from the tip of her hat to the toes of her boots. Her nose was hooked and her fingernails were like old bent knives. Long grey hair straggled over her shoulders. Her eyes glowed red, like hot coals. On top of all that, lying across her lap was a whip! A long leather whip that appeared to be twitching at the tip. To the horror of the Familiars, a Crow with ink black feathers squatted on her shoulder. It wore a pink ribbon around its neck, tied in a bow — a small, feminine touch that didn't match its black beady little eyes.

Slowly the Witch crooked a single bony finger. With quite a bit of nudging and pushing, everyone reluctantly filed down the aisle.

Pongwiffy held back until last. The Plan Of Resistance was now in operation. She waited until the rest were assembled at the foot of the stage, then sauntered down the aisle, really taking her time. Hugo tried to look casual too, but his eyes never left the Crow.

Everyone squinted up at the stage. There was deadly silence. And then —

'Grandwitch Crackwippy,' said the new Witch in

a slow, cracked voice like a bag of rusty nails being dragged through shards of glass. 'That's me. And this is Christine.'

The Familiars stared at Christine.

Christine said, 'Seen enough?'

This is the ultimate girl put-down line. It's always delivered in a sharp, challenging way that boys don't like. The Familiars looked away and affected a sudden interest in the cracks running across the ceiling.

'The Broom's called Gnasher,' said Crackwippy. 'But your Brooms will address him as "Sir".'

Everyone glanced uneasily over their shoulder at Gnasher, who sneered and cracked his twiggy knuckles.

'So,' went on Crackwippy, in her horrible, rasping drawl. 'Here you all are. Look at 'em, Christine. What a sorry bunch.'

This proved too much for Macabre. She dismounted from Rory and stood with clenched fists.

'Excuse *me*! *Sorry bunch?*'

Crackwippy fixed her with a hot red stare.

'You'll be Macabre,' she said. 'The mouthy one.'

A gasp went up. Nobody ever called Macabre mouthy. Well, not to her face. Macabre gaped like a fish.

'Go on, Macabre,' muttered Pongwiffy. 'You're not taking that, right?'

To her discomfort, the glowing gaze turned on *her*. Christine's head turned too, and Hugo tried to squeeze behind Pongwiffy's ear.

'You'll be the smelly one,' said Crackwippy. 'There's always a smelly one.'

Normally Pongwiffy would have jumped to the defence of her unique smell, of which she was rightly proud, but there was something very sinister about those hot red eyes.

'I suppose we should introduce ourselves,' trilled Sharkadder, trying to break the tension. 'Shall I begin? I'm . . .'

'No.' Crackwippy cut her off. 'We've done our homework. We know who you are, don't we, Christine?'

'Yeah,' sneered Christine. 'A loada losers.'

The Familiars nearly died. A girl Crow? Calling them *losers*?

'Zat not polite,' ventured Hugo, from behind Pongwiffy's ear. Brave words, but his squeak had a nervous crack.

'Shut your mouth, rodent squirt,' said Christine.

'Now listen up,' said Crackwippy. 'I've had a long flight and I haven't unpacked yet. I shan't get cracking until morning. I just wanted to get a sense of the rubbish I'm working with.'

Witches and Familiars alike cast aghast looks at each other. Were they to just stand there and take it?

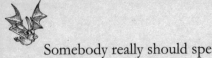

Somebody really should speak up . . .

'Why are we here, then?' asked Pongwiffy. 'If you know who we are and don't want to tell us anything until tomorrow, why are we wasting time?'

'Because,' said Crackwippy, 'I'm Grandwitch — and Grandwitches do what they like. You've probably noticed I've got a whip.'

'Sourmuddle doesn't need a whip,' said Pongwiffy. 'She encourages discussion around a table. She usually overrules us at the end, but we always get a say.'

'Not my style,' said Crackwippy. 'I don't do *tables*. Things don't get *discussed*, they get *done*. And because you've got so much to say for yourself, smelly one, I shall expect you at my cottage at daybreak tomorrow. The rest of you can have a lie-in and be there by six.'

Six o'clock in the morning?

There were two *clonks* as Bonidle and her Sloth Familiar slumped to the floor.

'Don't be late,' warned Crackwippy. 'I'm not happy with the accommodation. I'm making some changes. You!' She stabbed a finger at Greymatter. 'Bring a pencil. I shall be dictating new rules.'

'What about us?' enquired Filth. 'Do the Familiars have to come?'

'Oh yes. Christine'll take charge of you,' said Crackwippy.

'Oh, man,' said Filth brokenly.

'That'll be all,' said Crackwippy. 'For now. Go home to beddy-byes and get some sleep. You'll need it.'

And she raised the whip.

CRRRRAAAACK!

Lightning flashed – Crackwippy, Christine, Gnasher and the black throne vanished! The green light snapped off, the doors swung open in their usual unhurried way, and the Hall was back to normal.

'The eyes,' whispered Sludgegooey into the silence.

'The pink ribbon,' said Dudley.

'The hair!' shuddered Sharkadder. 'That terrible *hair*!'

'The *beak* on her,' groaned Barry. 'The *claws*.'

'The whip,' said Macabre. She shook her head. 'I dinnae like the look o' that whip.'

'Catch me getting up at daybreak tomorrow,' said Pongwiffy. 'Not likely.'

Nobody said a word. Even Hugo was strangely silent.

Pongwiffy tried to whip up a bit of interest in the Plan of Resistance, but everyone just drifted off into the night and she found herself talking to an empty hall.

Chapter
Four

It was the following morning. The sun was rising over Crag Hill where the Witches sometimes hold their Meetings. Right now, there were no Witches to be seen. Just Goblins. Halfway up the hill, the entire gasping Gaggle clustered around a large wooden sign. It read:

HELPFUL BOB'S ESSENTIAL
NECESSITIES EMPORIUM

A painted arrow pointed to a narrow track winding off to the right.

'You're sure this is it?' panted Hog.

'Yes,' wheezed Plugugly, examining the card from the Thing in the Moonmad T-shirt and carefully comparing it with the sign. 'De strokes is de same, see?'

'I'm restin',' announced Slopbucket. 'Me feet hurt.' He flung himself on to the scrubby grass, bashing his head on the signpost, which was the only obstacle for miles around. 'Ow!'

'We all wants a *rest*,' said Hog.

He was right. They did. That's because they had

walked for *a whole day and night*. Why? Because Plugugly got the directions wrong. Instead of turning left, he had started off by turning right.

They had gone for *miles*. They were off the map and into another land altogether before they realised. Then there was a fight. That took a while. Not as long as retracing their steps, though.

'Let's follow the arrow, then,' yawned Lardo. 'Is it the pointy end or the blunt one?'

'Pointy,' said Plugugly.

''Ow d'you know?' argued Sproggit. 'You don't even know left from right. 'Ow d'you know it's the pointy end?'

''Cos de udder end leads off de cliff.'

'Oh, yeah. See what you mean.'

Following the pointy end, Plugugly led them off. After a few paces, they turned a corner –

And there it was! *Helpful Bob's Essential Necessities Emporium*. A tiny wooden hut, all on its own, right on the edge of a cliff. Well, hut's too grand a word. It was little more than a box, really, with a counter and a sign saying OPEN. Behind, there was nothing but thin air and a sickening drop.

Leaning on the counter was a short bearded man wearing neat overalls and a tie.

Plugugly stopped, and everyone collided in concertina fashion.

The man looked up and said with a bright, sunny

smile, 'Good day, gentlemen. Helpful Bob at your service.'

The Goblins looked at each other and sniggered a bit. *Gentlemen?*

'Is dis de Hessessenshul Ne—' Plugugly broke off and glanced sideways at Sproggit. 'You know, dat word.'

'Necessities,' said Helpful Bob. 'Yes, this is the Essential Necessities Emporium.'

'I 'eard you sells – stuff,' said Plugugly doubtfully. He wasn't too good at spatial awareness, but even he could see that the hut was hardly big enough for Bob, let alone stuff.

'I do,' agreed Helpful Bob. 'Essential *stuff*, as you put it. All in the warehouse out the back. You just place your order and I bring it out. If it's not in stock, I can ring and get it from my cousin.'

'What ware'ouse?' chipped in Sproggit, peering around the back of the Emporium. 'I don't see no ware'ouse.'

'Ah,' said Bob. 'But you're not in the retail trade, are you, sir? Now then. What are you gents after this fine day?'

'A bed,' said Plugugly and held his breath.

'Uh-huh,' said Helpful Bob. 'Any particular kind?'

'Big,' said Plugugly. 'Wiv bouncy springs. An' a fick mattress. An' white sheets an' fluffy pillers.'

'Uh-huh.' Bob pulled out a pad and wrote it down.

'An' a Goblin Rangers bedspread!' exploded Sproggit, unable to contain himself.

'Yay!' shouted the others. 'Goblin Rangers! Yay!'

'Uh-huh,' said Bob, scribbling away.

'It's gotta fit in the cave,' added Eyesore. 'Go in the gap an' not take up all the room.'

There fell an expectant silence. All eyes were on Bob.

'Right,' said Bob. 'You're after a well-sprung king-size with a decent mattress, clean bedding and a Goblin Rangers bedspread. It needs to be carried through a small hole into a cave. And once in, it mustn't be in the way.'

The Goblins nodded, looking excited. All except Plugugly. As Bob ran through the list of bed requirements, Plugugly realised it was too much to hope for. Surely such a bed could never exist.

'Have you considered underneath storage drawers?' enquired Helpful Bob. 'Costs a little more, but very useful when there are space limitations.'

What was this?

'Of course, there's no money down immediately. Special opening deal. But I strongly recommend the drawers. And maybe a built-in reading lamp?'

'You mean – you got one? You really got a *bed*?' gasped Plugugly.

'Not in the warehouse. Sold the last one last night.'

Plugugly's dream shattered into a thousand pieces.

'But I can get you another,' added Bob. 'I'll call my cousin – he'll bring it round.'

The pieces flew back together again, like an instant jigsaw puzzle.

'It might take a while for him to get it over,' said Bob.

''Ow long?' begged Plugugly. 'Like – *years?*'

'Oh no. Shall we say – in an hour from now? I can recommend a pleasant little cafe where you can wait in comfort. Down the hill, turn left, you can't miss it. Run by a nice old lady called Mrs Muffin. Tell her I sent you and you'll get free toasted tea cakes.'

The Gaggle couldn't believe their ears. They were getting a bed! It would arrive in an hour! They didn't even have to pay! And they could eat free tea cakes while they waited!

Life had never been so good.

Chapter Five

Grandwitch Sourmuddle was fond of her cottage. Roses twined around the front door, which was painted a cheerful yellow. There were window boxes full of geraniums and the garden was a riot of colour. It was nice inside too, with comfy armchairs and polished side tables and china ornaments.

Well, that's what it was usually like. Right now, it was like a building site.

Bendyshanks, Sludgegooey, Ratsnappy and Scrofula were trampling all over the garden, pulling up flowers and tossing them into a wheelbarrow. Propped against the hedge were tall, spiked cacti, scratchy thorn bushes and bags of poisonous toadstools waiting to be planted.

Their Familiars were helping. Steve was marking out the positions for the cacti. Filth was in charge of the wheelbarrow, making endless trips to the large skip parked outside the gate. Vernon was smashing empty plant pots with a hammer and Barry was up a ladder, pulling at the climbing rose with his beak.

Macabre was painting the front door black, while Rory took short runs at the pretty cherry tree by the gate. The trunk was splintering and blossom rained down like pink snow. When the petals stuck to the wet door, Macabre just painted over them.

The Brooms had formed a chain gang. Overseen by Gnasher, they were passing furniture through the kitchen window. Chairs, tables, wardrobes, even Sourmuddle's precious spellovision set – they all ended up in the skip. Surrounded by her flock of Bats, Gaga was leaping up and down on top, pressing it down to make extra room.

Inside the cottage, there was more industry. Watched by IdentiKit and CopiCat, the twins stood teetering on the draining board in the kitchen, taking down Sourmuddle's lace curtains. Behind them, Bonidle was drifting around collecting up Sourmuddle's beloved china and dropping it into a sack, held open by the Sloth.

Sharkadder came bursting through the back door with Dudley in tow, a tray in her hands and lipstick all awry.

'I've got it!' she panted. 'I've done her breakfast! Just like she ordered!'

The twins and Bonidle paused in their tasks and looked down at the tray. Sharkadder had surpassed herself. There were muffins, crumpets and rolls. There was buttered toast with a side dish of straw-berry jam. There was a pot of tea and a bowl of sugar lumps. There were bacon rashers, sausages and eggs. There was a bowl of lice bites and a jug of milk. She had thought of everything.

'You'd better take it in, hadn't she, Bag?' said Agglebag.

'Yes, Ag. She's been asking for it,' agreed Bagaggle.

'In there, is she?' Sharkadder glanced nervously at the parlour door.

'Yes,' chorused the twins. 'Go on.'

Sharkadder gave the door a nervous little push with the toe of her shoe. It creaked open and she sidled in.

It was dark in the parlour. Dark – and much changed! Everything had been removed. Every side table, every chair. There was a blank space where the sofa used to be. There were pale places on the walls where Sourmuddle's family portraits had once hung. Even the carpet had been taken up to reveal ancient black floorboards.

The only item in the room was the horrible throne. It was placed directly before the window overlooking the trampled garden. In it sat Crackwippy, whip across her lap and Christine on her shoulder.

Beside the throne stood a frazzled Greymatter, pad in hand, clearly in the middle of making a very, *very* long list. Speks hovered beside her with a selection of pencils in his beak.

Sharkadder tiptoed across the bare floorboards. She stopped before the throne and attempted to genuflect. The plate of toast slid to one side and a piece fell on the floor, butter side down.

'Sorry,' gulped Sharkadder.

Crackwippy's red eyes surveyed the tray. 'Call that breakfast?' she sneered.

'Rubbish,' agreed Christine. Her baleful eyes were on Dudley. 'What you staring at?'

'Shall I take it away?' quavered Sharkadder.

'No, pass it over,' said Crackwippy. 'I suppose I'll try it. But next time, I want black treacle. Strawberry's for wimps. Get out.'

Sharkadder and Dudley got out at double speed.

'You!' Crackwippy pointed at Greymatter, who quailed. 'On with the New Rules. I'll continue while I'm eating. Rule Twelve. *All Cottages To Be Painted Black*. Rule Thirteen. *All Wands To Be Handed In Until Further Notice*. Rule Fourteen. *All Piggy Banks To Be Emptied And The Contents Delivered To Me*. Rule Fifteen. *All Latecomers To Be Severely Punished*. Talking of which –' She broke off and gave an unpleasant chuckle. 'Here comes the smelly one. That's it, smelly one. Take your time. Make my day.'

Through the window, Pongwiffy could be seen walking slowly up the path with Hugo on her hat. She was attempting to look casual, but you could tell that she was shocked.

Sharkadder came rushing round the side of the cottage, Dudley at her heels and hanky to her eyes.

'Hey!' said Pongwiffy. 'Where are you going? You're supposed to be *slow*, that's what we agreed . . .'

But Sharkadder was already gone. The sound of her weeping died away.

Pongwiffy avoided the wet black front door. Macabre grimly dipped her brush into the pot and said nothing.

Pongwiffy went round to the back and entered the kitchen, where the twins were still unhooking curtains and Bonidle was emptying the shelves. More tins of black paint were lined up against the wall.

'What's going on?' demanded Pongwiffy.

'We're clearing the kitchen,' whispered Agglebag. 'Got to make room for her cauldron and her bottles of poison. And her collection of cobwebs. When everything's out, we start painting the walls black.'

'*What?* Sourmuddle will go *mad*. What happened to the Plan of Resistance?'

'We decided against it,' mumbled Agglebag.

'She got the whip out,' muttered Bagaggle. 'She said she'd set fire to our hats.'

'Where have you been, Pongwiffy?' enquired Bonidle. 'You were supposed to arrive at daybreak. We've been here for *hours*.'

'Well,' said Pongwiffy, 'if you want to be her slaves, more fool you.'

'She's in the parlour,' said Bagaggle. 'She said you're to go in the moment you arrive.'

'Fine,' said Pongwiffy. 'She doesn't scare us, does she, Hugo?'

Hugo said nothing. He was thinking about Christine.

Pongwiffy knocked briskly on the parlour door and went in.

Crackwippy was enthroned in the dark, noisily chewing a mouthful of bacon. The tray sat on her lap, together with the whip.

'Out,' she commanded Greymatter. 'We'll continue later.'

Greymatter didn't need to be told twice, and neither did Speks.

'Come here, smelly one,' growled Crackwippy.

Pongwiffy approached the throne. Slowly, as the Plan of Resistance dictated.

'Think you're clever?' The hot red eyes did their boring thing. 'Trying to be *rebellious*, are we? Trying to get one over? Is that it?' Crackwippy picked up a crumpet and bit into it. '*No one* gets one over on me. Right, Christine?'

'Yeah, right,' said Christine, her wicked little eyes on Hugo. 'I'm gonna *peck* you, furball.'

'Let me tell you something,' went on Crackwippy. 'I've been doing this job a long time. See this?' She patted the whip on her lap, which seemed to wriggle. 'A Magic Whip. It's all-purpose. Like a Wand, but with more – *attitude*.' She took a slurp of tea. 'I'm going to lick you into shape. Not just you Witches. Everybody. Skeletons, Trolls, Ghouls and all the rest of 'em. From now on, *I Rule This Wood* and everyone needs to know it. Which is why you're going to carve the statue.'

'Pardon?' said Pongwiffy.

'You heard. It's your punishment for being late. You're to carve a mighty statue of me. In black marble. A glorious monument that'll cause fear and trembling to all who clap eyes on it. A perfect like-ness, at least three times my height, with a brass plaque at the bottom with my name on it. It's to be erected directly in front of Witchway Hall.'

'Now, wait a minute!' objected Pongwiffy. 'This is ridiculous. We don't know how to carve, do we, Hugo?'

'Then it'll be a challenge, won't it? And in case you're wondering, no Magic is to be used. You'll do it the hard way. I want a Grand Unveiling at midnight tonight and it had better be good. There'll be posters everywhere so there's no excuse for not attending. The marble's already there, along with your tools. I suggest you get cracking.' She glanced meaningfully at her whip. 'Or *I* will. I'll be sending Christine along to check up on you.'

'But . . .'

CRRRRAAAAACK!

The tray tumbled to the floor as the whip cracked! A flash of green light . . .

And a split second later, Pongwiffy and Hugo found themselves lying flat on their backs in front of Witchway Hall. Pongwiffy's hat was on fire and a distinct smell of singed whiskers wafted from Hugo. Both of them jumped up and began beating themselves out.

It was only when they had stopped smoking that they saw it. A massive chunk of black marble, towering over the glade! Next to it was a stepladder and a toolbag.

The new Supply didn't mess about.

It's all very well fooling around with plasticine, or even clay. But carving a giant statue from marble is a very different kettle of fish. Even with the right tools. The right tools, apparently, were chisels and hammers. Two of each – normal-sized ones for Pongwiffy and tiny ones for Hugo.

'Where shall we start?' asked Pongwiffy. 'Top or bottom?'

'Dunno.'

'I'll go up the ladder and start with the nose. You work at the bottom where the plaque has to go.'

'OK.'

Tools in hand, they approached the marble

mountain. Pongwiffy climbed the stepladder and stood wobbling at the top. She placed her chisel where she thought the nose should be and gave it a little tap with her hammer. The chisel skittered harmlessly to one side, making no impression whatsoever.

'Tap 'arder,' called up Hugo.

So Pongwiffy tapped harder. Still no joy.

'Give big bash,' suggested Hugo.

Pongwiffy drew back her arm and brought the hammer down with all her strength. It missed the chisel altogether and connected with the marble. A large chunk splintered off and fell down, narrowly missing Hugo's foot.

'Hey! Votch out!'

'Sorry,' said Pongwiffy, examining the hole she had created. 'But at least I made an impact. Brute force, that's what's needed. *You* try.'

'OK.' Hugo held his tiny chisel in position, drew back his hammer and gave it his all. A crack appeared at the base and ran almost halfway up.

'Careful!' scolded Pongwiffy. 'You don't know your own strength!'

'Ya, I do,' said Hugo happily. Well, he did. He was really strong, for a Hamster.

'Right,' said Pongwiffy. 'Let's get bashing.'

Both of them attacked the marble with renewed vigour.

Thwack! Bash! Thwack!

Bits of marble pinged all over the place. Black, gritty dust rained down into their eyes. Pongwiffy whacked away, and another large chunk broke off and came crashing down. This one *did* fall on Hugo's foot.

'Ow!' wailed Hugo, dancing around. 'Ow! Ow! Ow!'

'Stop complaining,' said Pongwiffy. 'I think I've got the nose sorted. What d'you think?'

Rubbing his foot, Hugo stared up to where a long, thin, vaguely nose-like shape had emerged.

'Not bad,' he said doubtfully.

'It's not, is it? But it's not quite hooked enough. One more little tap, and it'll be perfect.'

'Leave it,' advised Hugo.

'No, no. I'm getting the hang now. Just a gentle little tap, here at the end . . .'

Pongwiffy angled her chisel, drew back her hammer and gave it a little tap. The entire nose fell off. Hugo dived clear just before it reached the ground, where it stuck quivering like an arrow.

'Bother!' sighed Pongwiffy, climbing back down the ladder. 'I s'pose that's what you'd call a nosedive.'

They both stood back and examined the marble lump. It looked much the same as it did at the beginning, except for the new holes.

'It's hopeless, isn't it?' said Pongwiffy.

'Ya.'

'What are we going to do?'

'Dunno.'

'Let's have a rest while we think about it.'

'But *Christine* comink . . .'

'Yes, but she's not here yet.'

'OK.'

They flopped down under a tree on a handy log. Pongwiffy fished around in her cardigan pocket, hoping to find something like a fluffy toffee or some old cake. She said, 'Oooh. What have we here? I'd forgotten about this.'

It was the card. The card that they had found two nights ago, by the side of the trail.

'*Helpful Bob's Essential Necessities Emporium*,' mused Pongwiffy. 'Hey! You don't suppose they'd have a statue of a Supply Grandwitch, do you?'

'Mmm.' Hugo sounded doubtful. 'It long shot.'

'But suppose they do? It's says here, *Buy now, pay later*. Look, there's a list of things they sell. My word! This is impressive! Everything from clothes pegs to islands in the sun. It doesn't actually mention statues, but it's worth a try. Crackwippy wouldn't have to know. We could claim it was all our own work.'

'Vot about ze green spots? She know you tell lies.'

'You can do the talking. Look, just pop along and

ask. It's halfway up Crag Hill. There's a map on the back, see?'

'But zat *miles*!'

'So take the Broom. You'll be there in no time.'

'But *Christine* . . .'

'I'll deal with Christine. Go on.'

'OK,' said Hugo. He didn't much fancy flying all the way to Crag Hill on a fool's errand. But then again, he didn't fancy Christine either.

'While you're gone, I'll keep chipping so it looks like we're making progress,' said Pongwiffy. 'Hurry up.'

Hugo went scuttling off.

Pongwiffy sat back and stretched her legs out. She was just about to go rummaging through her pockets again, when a voice from above said, 'Where's the rodent gone?' Christine was staring down from a branch.

'Cut his paw with the chisel,' lied Pongwiffy. 'Gone for a plaster.'

'Wimp,' sneered Christine. She pointed a claw. 'What's with the green spots?'

'Allergic to Crows,' said Pongwiffy nastily.

They glared at each other.

'Why are you sitting down?' asked Christine.

'I'm thinking,' said Pongwiffy, gazing at the lump of marble. 'And looking. You can't rush artistic vision.'

'I'm telling her you're sitting down,' said Christine. 'I'm telling her you're just making a mess.'

'Tell her what you like,' said Pongwiffy.

They glared at each other a bit more. Then Christine gave a harsh croak and flew away.

Chapter
Six

'Yes, sir?' said Helpful Bob, leaping up. 'How can I help?'

'Is you Bob?' enquired Hugo, climbing off the Broom.

'I am, sir. After something special?'

'Statue,' said Hugo, not too hopefully.

'Uh-huh.' Bob reached for his pencil. 'What sort of statue?'

'Statue of Vitch. Very ugly. Got Magic Vip.'

'A Magic Whip, I see.' Bob noted it down.

'Got scary eyes. Red vuns.'

'Sounds to me like . . .' Bob squinted into the distance, then snapped his fingers. 'Grandwitch Crackwippy.'

''Ow you know zat?' enquired Hugo, amazed.

'Old customer of mine. As a matter of fact, I sold her the whip. Now, what do you want it made of? Ice? Chocolate? Cheese?'

'Black marble.'

'Ah. Well, you're lucky there. If you'd wanted a *chocolate* one I couldn't have helped you. But I just happen to have a black marble one in the warehouse.'

'*You do?*'

'Certainly. It's even got a name plaque. Where's it being delivered?'

'Outside Vitchvay Hall,' said Hugo, weak with relief.

'Excellent. I'll pop out the back and put a sticker on. It'll be with you in under the hour.'

And with that, Bob vanished. The Emporium was empty.

Hugo and the Broom stared at each other. Then the Broom gave a happy little skip, and Hugo turned the first of what would be a great many somersaults.

Much, much later, as the sun was going down, seven battered, blistered, exhausted Goblins came trudging back up Crag Hill. Believe it or not, they had got lost again. Plugugly's fault as usual. Instead of turning left, he had gone right and they had spent hours tramping along pointless paths. Sproggit had accused him of being rubbish and there had been strong words and much rolling around in the dirt.

'Just fink,' panted Eyesore. 'We could be eatin' free tea cakes right now.'

'Or even *four* tea cakes,' gasped Lardo.

'Dere's de sign,' puffed Plugugly, pointing. 'Nearly dere.'

'No fanks to you,' mumbled Sproggit. But not

too loudly. He was too tired to contemplate another fight.

'Think it'll be there waitin' for us?' asked Eyesore.

'Dunno,' said Plugugly as they set off along the winding little path. 'Prob'ly not, knowin' our luck.'

But he was wrong.

The Gaggle rounded the bend – and there it was! The Bed! Parked right outside the *Essential Necessities Emporium*, catching the last of the sun's orange rays.

'Ooooh!' breathed Slopbucket. 'It's – *boooooootiful*!'

And it was. The bed was everything they wanted. It was big. It was luxurious. It almost certainly had bouncy springs and a thick mattress and white sheets and fluffy pillows, although you couldn't see them because they were covered by a Goblin Rangers bedspread!

'Yay!' shrieked Sproggit, punching the air. 'Goblin Rangers! Yay!'

''Evening, gentlemen,' called Helpful Bob. There he was, leaning on the counter, smiling his pleasant smile.

Plugugly dragged his eyes from the bed with difficulty. Like the rest of the Gaggle, he was quite choked up.

'A little later than we said,' observed Bob. '*Ten hours* later, in fact. But luckily, I'm still open. So. Is it to your liking?'

'Yes,' croaked Plugugly. 'Oh, *yes*!'

'Storage drawers underneath. And of course your built-in reading lamp.'

'Yes,' breathed Plugugly.

'Well, if everything's in order, it's yours. Take it.'

The Gaggle looked at each other. Take it?

''Ow?' asked Hog.

'Well, it's got little wheels, so you can push it back up to the main trail. Then you can guide it down the hill. It'll roll under its own momentum.'

'Dat sounds tricky,' said Plugugly doubtfully. The bed was big. The bed was heavy, you could tell. Heavy and awkward.

'Afraid I can't deliver it,' said Bob sadly. 'The delivery boy's on another job. I could do it tomorrow.'

'But we wants it *now*,' wailed Plugugly.

'It's all down to pushing it, then,' said Bob.

He was right. It was.

'It's horrible,' said Pongwiffy, staring up at the glowering statue that towered above them, giving out bad vibes and generally dominating the glade. 'It's her, though.'

The statue had materialised out of thin air mere seconds after Hugo had arrived back. It was indeed the spitting image of Grandwitch Crackwippy, but three times bigger. One arm was raised threateningly in the air, brandishing the whip.

'I know,' beamed Hugo.

'Eyes, nose, hair, whip, name plaque, everything. And you didn't even have to *pay*?'

'Nope. Buy now, pay later.'

'Perfect. Now all we have to do is get rid of that.' Pongwiffy pointed to the battered chunk of original marble that lay alongside. 'I'll use a disappearing spell.' She fished around under her cardigan and produced her Wand.

Hugo covered his eyes. Pongwiffy's spells tended to be hit and miss.

'Listen now to what I say,
Chunk of marble, go away!'

And to the amazement of them both – it worked!

'Well, that's sorted,' said Pongwiffy, pleased with herself. 'Now we need to find something to drape over the statue. My bedsheet'll do. Let's go back to the hovel and celebrate with supper.'

'Vait.' Hugo pointed. 'I sink ve got company.'

Two Trolls had come out of the trees and were loitering at the edge of the glade.

'What do you want?' challenged Pongwiffy.

'Nothin',' said the biggest Troll. 'Come to see the statue.'

'Well, it's not being unveiled until midnight.'

'How come we can see it now, then?' asked the smaller one.

'Because it's not got its *veil* on yet, stupid –' She broke off and whirled round. Suspicious crackling sounds were coming from the undergrowth. 'Halt!' said Pongwiffy. 'Who goes there?'

'I not zere,' said Hugo, puzzled. 'I *'ere.*'

'Not you! I said, *Who Goes There?*'

The bushes shook, and out stepped a strangely assorted group consisting of a Skeleton, a Tree Demon, a Werewolf and a Gnome. All of them looked a bit shifty. The Skeleton had a pail of whitewash. The Gnome was trying to hide a jar of yellow paint behind his back.

'What are you lot doing?' snapped Pongwiffy.

'Just out walking,' said the Skeleton. 'Taking the air, admiring the view.'

'A likely story,' said Pongwiffy. 'You've come to do horrible things to the statue, haven't you?'

'Statue?' said the Skeleton. 'What statue?' He stared past Pongwiffy and gave a theatrical start. 'Oh my! A statue!'

'Hey!' interrupted Hugo. 'Vot zem two doink?'

The Trolls had sneaked up to the statue. The big one was standing on the smaller one's shoulders, hastily chalking a red moustache on the upper lip.

'Get *down*!' shouted Pongwiffy. 'Hugo, stop him!'

Hugo rushed forward. The big Troll quickly leapt down and the pair of them lumbered off into the night.

'Go home,' Pongwiffy ordered the Skeleton and his friends. 'Come back at midnight, in a proper manner.'

She watched them slink off into the bushes. They didn't go far though. You could hear them rustling.

'I suppose we should stay and stand guard,' said Pongwiffy, staring thoughtfully at the red moustache. 'Who knows what might happen while we're gone?'

'Vot, go vizzout supper?'

'Well, no. Obviously, we can't go without *supper.*'

'Zen let's go.'

And off they went for supper, which consisted of three large helpings of skunk stew, washed down with a great many cups of bogwater.

Halfway up Crag Hill, the full moon poured silver light upon the scene below.

The Goblins were clustered around the bed. It had taken for ever to push it up to the main trail. It had jammed in bushes, got stuck in tree roots and proved almost impossible to manoeuvre. But the Goblins had persevered and, after a lot of sweating, panting and arguing, had finally succeeded.

'Should be easier now,' wheezed Eyesore. 'Wider, ain't it. Less bumps.'

'Steep, though,' said Hog, eyeing the trail uneasily.

'Dat's good,' said Plugugly. 'It's *good* dat it's steep.

Like Bob said, it'll roll. Under its own mom-mom-mom . . .' – Sproggit began looking around for a stick – 'mom-mom-*entum*!'

'So what do we do now?' asked Lardo.

'We pushes,' said Plugugly. 'Like dis.'

He marched round, stationed himself behind the headboard, reached out a finger and gave the bed a little push. Just a little push. Just to demonstrate.

You can guess what happens next, right?

Chapter Seven

It was almost midnight. In Witchway Wood, the glade was rapidly filling up as a result of the posters that had appeared everywhere. They read:

**MIDNIGHT TONIGHT.
GRAND UNVEILING OF MY STATUE.
BE THERE OR ELSE!
GRANDWITCH CRACKWIPPY**

Despite the bossy wording, curiosity had won the day. Everyone was keen to inspect the new Supply. The Skeletons and Trolls were out in force. The Tree Demon was there, and the Werewolf, and the Thing in the Moonmad T-shirt. Two Yetis had set up a stall and were doing a brisk trade in hot dogs. All eyes were on the statue, currently shrouded in Pongwiffy's disgusting bedsheet.

Pongwiffy and Hugo hovered in its shadow, keeping suspiciously quiet.

'When's it startin'?' enquired a Zombie.

'Soon,' said Pongwiffy shortly.

'I scared,' whispered Hugo. He looked a bit pale around the pouches. 'I sink ve get in big trou—'

54

'*Left, right, left, right, left, right . . .*'

There was no mistaking that voice.

Into the glade trooped the Familiars. A day of enforced cottage vandalism and Crow abuse had beaten them into submission. Their spirit was broken. The Crow herself flapped above their heads, occasionally swooping down to give the stragglers a spiteful peck.

'Oh!' gasped Hugo. 'Zat so *humiliatink*!'

'*Halt!*' commanded Christine, and the Familiars halted. Then she turned to the gaping crowd and said, 'Got a problem?'

That was just for starters. No one was prepared for the main course.

CRASH! That was a peal of thunder.

FLASH! That was lightning.

CRAAAAAACK! That was a whip!

And from out of the trees came the new Grandwitch with a line of shamefaced Witches shuffling behind.

The crowd drew back. There was something about the red eyes and flying hair. And the whip, of course. Nobody wanted to get in the way of that.

Crackwippy held up a hand, and the Witches trailed to a halt.

Slowly, Crackwippy walked to the veiled mound. Christine flew on to her shoulder and treated the onlookers to her baleful stare. Somewhere, a

Gnome toddler started to cry.

Crackwippy turned her hot red gaze on the crowd.

'Grandwitch Crackwippy,' she rasped. 'That's me. I'm the new boss around here.'

There were mutters of alarm. Some of them sounded rebellious. A Troll waved a fist and shouted, 'Like heck!'

'Shut your gobs,' said Christine in her charming way, and the mutters died away.

'I have assembled you all here,' went on Crackwippy, 'because I am about to unveil my specially commissioned statue. It is a symbol of my absolute power. The moment you set eyes on it, you will fall to your knees.'

Nobody said a word. Those present who didn't happen to possess knees – Snakes, Bats and Birds, mainly – thought about saying something. But they didn't.

'Right.' Crackwippy glared at Pongwiffy. 'Remove the veil.'

Pongwiffy and Hugo looked at each other. Then they reached out and gave a yank. The sheet slithered to the ground.

'Behold my terrible face!' thundered Crackwippy.

A gasp went up. It should have been a gasp of awe. After all, the statue was very lifelike. Well, it was once.

It now had a red moustache, a matching beard and chalked-on spectacles. The pointy hat had clown-like yellow bobbles painted on. Someone had twined a string of sausages around the neck. A scrap of paper had been stuck over the name plaque with one word on it. The word was:

TWITWIPPY

Crackwippy stared at the statue for a long moment. Then her gaze fell on Pongwiffy.

'Banishment,' she said. 'Banishment from the Coven. Long overdue, I reckon. Set her to work in a laundry. What d'you think, Christine?'

'Yeah, nice one,' agreed Christine.

There was a sharp intake of breath from the crowd. Pongwiffy? Banished? Sent to *work in a laundry*? Could there *be* a worse punishment?

'Noooooooo!' The anguished wail escaped from Sharkadder. 'Not *soooap*! It's too *cruuuuuel*!'

'Now, hang *on* . . .' began Pongwiffy, then quailed as Crackwippy raised her whip. Hugo braced himself.

'So this is where you've all got to,' said a familiar voice. And who should step out from behind the statue but –

Sourmuddle! Sourmuddle, with suitcase in hand and Snoop at her heels. No sign of the ice skates.

There were howls of delighted relief from Witches and Familiars alike. Excited whispering broke out amongst the watching crowd. Now what?

'I'm back,' announced Sourmuddle. 'And not before time. I've just been by my cottage and quite frankly, I'm appalled! My geraniums! My furniture! My spellovision! My lovely yellow door! Who's responsible?'

Delight and relief gave way to shame. Those responsible shuffled their feet and hung their heads. And then —

'*She* is,' said Pongwiffy, pointing at Crackwippy. '*She* made them do it.'

Sourmuddle treated Crackwippy to the sort of look normally reserved for something crawling out of a lettuce sandwich. Crackwippy leered.

'Yellow,' she drawled. 'Not my style.'

'Where's my Broom?' snapped Sourmuddle. 'Where's Stumpy?'

Crackwippy gave a shrug. 'In the shed. Refused to obey orders. Gnasher's guarding it.'

'How *dare* you!' hissed Sourmuddle. 'Who do you think you are?'

'She's Grandwitch Crackwippy,' chipped in Christine. 'And she can do what she l— *eeeek!*'

There was a strangled squawk, and Christine vanished in mid-sentence. The pink ribbon floated down and was caught by the Thing in the

Moonmad T-shirt, who ate it.

A huge cheer went up from the Familiars.

'See that?' muttered Pongwiffy. 'Didn't even need her Wand. Amazing.'

'So it's like that, is it?' snarled Crackwippy dangerously.

'It is,' agreed Sourmuddle. 'And you know what happens next?'

But she didn't get the chance to explain, because something happened next that no one was expecting! There came a rumbling noise, accompanied by crashings, squeakings and tinklings – and into the glade charged –

The bed! But, oh dear. It wasn't the bed we remember.

It had come on a long journey, that runaway bed. Down Crag Hill, picking up speed as it went, zooming straight into Witchway Wood, smashing down small trees and scattering pillows in its wake. The bedspread was buried under a coating of leaves, twigs and dirt. Somewhere along the way it had shed the storage drawers and the reading lamp. It was a *mess*.

Everyone dived for cover as it hurtled across the glade. The bed might have been a mess, but it was a *fast* mess. Could anything halt it?

SMASH!

The statue could. Mind you, it paid. As the bed

careered into it, it slowly toppled over and crashed to the ground, exploding into a million pieces. The head rolled into a bush. The whip snapped in two. Bits of black marble rained down on the horrified crowd.

Only Sourmuddle and Crackwippy remained where they were. Sourmuddle looked vaguely surprised. Crackwippy's face could have melted icebergs.

The bed rolled a little further, finally shuddering to a halt against the Hall doors.

There was a long, long pause.

'Hmm,' said Sourmuddle. '*Interesting*. Right, where was I? What am I about to do next, Snoop?'

'Get rid of the rubbish?'

'That's it.'

And Sourmuddle snapped her fingers.

Quite some time later, Pongwiffy and Hugo sat in her hovel waiting for the kettle to boil.

'Did you *see* her, though?' said Pongwiffy for the tenth time. 'She just snapped her fingers – and no more Crackwippy. *Pfff*! Gone, just like that.'

'Ya, I saw.'

'She's going to send a stiff report to the Board and old Crackwippy'll lose her job.'

'Let's 'ope so,' said Hugo. 'She *nasty*.'

'It just goes to show. There are a lot worse

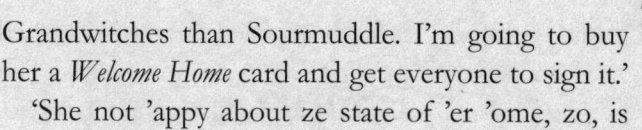

Grandwitches than Sourmuddle. I'm going to buy her a *Welcome Home* card and get everyone to sign it.'

'She not 'appy about ze state of 'er 'ome, zo, is she?' said Hugo doubtfully. 'You need a *Sorry Ve Turn Your Nice Cottage Into Scary Slum* card.'

'Oh, poo! She'll have it back to its old self by tomorrow.'

'Vhy she come back so soon?' asked Hugo, hopping down and scuttling to the sink for cups.

'Had a row with her sister. They've never got on. And she couldn't get the hang of winter sports. Tobogganed off a cliff, fell through the thin ice and got nipped by a moose. So she came home.'

'Vhere she belong,' said Hugo happily.

'Yes. So everything's back to normal. Goodbye, Crackwippy.'

'Goodbye, Christine!' whooped Hugo, and did a little tap dance in the sink. 'Now ve all boys togezzer again! Yippee!'

Pongwiffy watched him, grinning broadly, and said, 'Put six sugars in my bogwater, Hugo. I'm in a wonderful mood!'

And she was, too. Until the bill for the statue arrived.

Epilogue

In her perfectly tidy cottage, Grandwitch Sourmuddle is dashing off an angry letter to the Board. It has words like 'power-mad dictator', 'ludicrous whip', 'insolent crow' and 'ruined geraniums'. Ink spatters from her furious pen and little flames flicker around the edges of the paper. Things don't look good for Crackwippy or Christine. At the very least they'll get a ticking off. Let's hope the whip gets confiscated.

In the cave, the Goblins are in their usual pile. Plugugly is at the bottom, being the mattress. For once, they are sleeping peacefully: a combination of the long trudge home, disappointment about losing the bed and arguments about whose fault it was. Let's leave them snoring. They need their strength for tomorrow morning, when they, too, will receive a bill. It's going to be a big one. Beds like that don't come cheap.

And Helpful Bob? Right now, he is standing in the doorway of his warehouse. He is rubbing his hands and smiling.

The Great Pasta Disaster

Welcome to the weird and wonderful world of Grubtown where the mayor, Flabby Gomez, is knitting himself a new house and the chief of police, Grabby Hanson, is forever taking things (though he *always* gives them back, and often arrests himself). It's a bonkers town where EVERYONE loves ducks except, of course, for the duck-hating Fox family, and where floppy lettuce can lead to MASSIVE explosions packing a pasta punch! Join Jilly Cheeter and her best friend Mango Claptrap as they wade their way through the silliest of tomato-sauce soaked mysteries!

First published for World Book Day 2010
by Faber and Faber Limited
Bloomsbury House, 74–77 Great Russell Street,
London WC1B 3DA

Typeset by Faber and Faber Limited
Printed in England by CPI Bookmarque, Croydon

All rights reserved
© Philip Ardagh, 2010
Illustrations © Jim Paillot, 2010

The right of Philip Ardagh to be identified as author of this work
has been asserted in accordance with Section 77 of the Copyright,
Designs and Patents Act 1988

*This book is sold subject to the condition that it shall not, by way of trade
or otherwise, be lent, resold, hired out or otherwise circulated without the
publisher's prior consent in any form of binding or cover other than that
in which it is published and without a similar condition including this
condition being imposed on the subsequent purchaser*

This is a work of fiction. Other than those clearly in the public
domain, all characters, businesses, places, properties, products,
organisations and even Grubtown itself are figments of the
author's imagination (with the possible exception of himself).
Any similarities to existing entities, past or present, are purely
coincidental and should not be inferred.

A CIP record for this book
is available from the British Library

ISBN 978–0–9562877–5–5

2 4 6 8 10 9 7 5 3 1

GRuBtoWN taLes
World Book Day Special

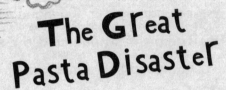

The Great Pasta Disaster

or

Exploding with Rage

by *Philip Ardagh*

Illustrated by Jim Paillot

ff

faber and faber

A bit about the author

Roald Dahl Funny Prize winner Philip Ardagh is the bestselling author of the Eddie Dickens adventures, currently in over 30 languages. He wrote BBC Radio's first truly interactive radio drama, collaborated with Sir Paul McCartney on his first children's book and is a 'regularly irregular' reviewer of children's books for the *Guardian*. Married with a son, he divides his time between Tunbridge Wells and Grubtown, where he cultivates his impressive beard.

A bit about Grubtown

You won't find Grubtown on any maps. The last time any mapmakers were sent anywhere near the place they were found a week later wearing nothing but pages from a telephone directory, and calling for their mothers. It's certainly a town and certainly grubby – except for the squeaky clean parts – but everything else we know about the place comes from Beardy Ardagh, town resident and author of these tales.

Grubtown TaLes were made possible
through the participation of the following
people, animals and organisations:

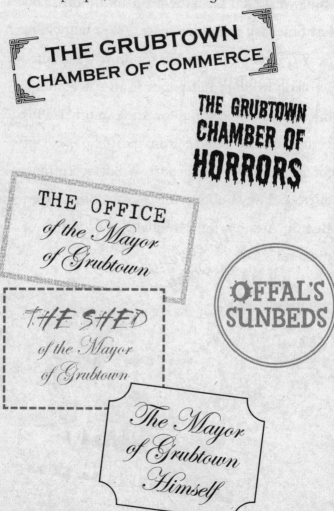

THE GRUBTOWN
CHAMBER OF COMMERCE

THE GRUBTOWN
CHAMBER OF
HORRORS

THE OFFICE
of the Mayor
of Grubtown

OFFAL'S
SUNBEDS

THE SHED
of the Mayor
of Grubtown

The Mayor
of Grubtown
Himself

THE GRUBTOWN
RIFLE
CLUB

THE GRUBTOWN
TRIFLE
(& JELLIES)
CLUB

THE GRUBTOWN
POLICE
DEPARTMENT

KILL ALL DUCKS

*Wretching's
Dairy*

JIP
THE PELICAN
★ ★ ★
GRUBTOWN'S
OFFICIAL
MASCOT

GRUBTOWN
COASTGUARD
& DECKCHAIR
DEPARTMENT

THE RUSTY
DOLPHIN CAFE

CONTENTS

Oi! Read this or else

I've absolutely no idea if this book is made from recycled paper because nobody has bothered to tell me. For all I know, this book is the very first thing a tree has been made into since *being* a tree, or it could have been made from recycled paper which was, until last week, a lorry load of old comedy paper hats, or a jumbo pack of disposable nappies for baby elephants.

What I *do* know is that the pictures in this story are 100 per cent recycled. If you've already read some **GRuBtoWN taLes** you might recognise some of them. If you go on to read some **GRuBtoWN taLes** after this World Book Day Special – and who, in their

right mind, wouldn't? – you might recognise some of them later.

The question I'd expect the less idiotic amongst you to be asking around about now is: '*Why, Beardy? Why? Why re-use old pictures instead of some lovely brand-spanking-new ones?*'

Because if we'd used *new* pictures, we would have had to have paid Jim to draw them and, instead, that money can be given to me to spend on good causes, such as 'Grow A Beard For Your Neighbour' or 'Be Very Tall This Christmas'.

See? I'm *always* thinking of other people.

(The very tall)

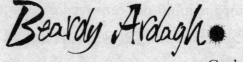

Grubtown

Chapter One
Floppy Lettuce!

The one good thing about being trapped under a pile of pasta and tomato sauce is that you can eat your way out. That's not something you can do if you're under a pile of rubble or a grand piano. When Premix Stipend was trapped in one of Chevvy Offal's sunbeds (in Offal's Sunbeds) she just had to grin and bear it, which is why she now has orange skin and her body makes a strange humming sound. Just hold this book up to your ear.

Hmmmmmmmmmmmmmm.

See what I mean?

She was also quite crispy for a while, but her crunchiest bits broke off in the end, and the rest of her has healed nicely. Mostly. (It's lucky I can't show you a picture of her. You might burst into tears.)

Pasta, which is really just a mix of flour and water, comes in all shapes and sizes. The shape of the pasta that Mrs Awning found herself under came in flat ribbon-like strips, which means that it was tagliatelle (pronounced *ta-lee-ah-telly*). It came flying out of a window and landed on her in a HUGE glumph. The glumph – a giant tangle – of pasta and sauce was about the size of one of the bushes at the entrance to Not-Nearly-So-Nice-Once-You-Come-through-the-Gates Park (which isn't nearly so nice once you come through the

gates) but if you've never been to Grubtown you'll have no idea how big I mean.

Mrs Awning – the one under the pasta, remember – often has accidents. There was the time she fell in the town well and out of an ambulance and got poked in the eye with a fishing rod and –

No, hang on.

I'll stop there.

This book isn't as long as the usual **GRuBtoWN taLes** and if I listed ALL her accidents – or just those in the past few years – I'd run out of pages.

The window out of which the glumph of pasta came flying was an upstairs window of Upstairs at Ample Saki's. This accident wasn't a part of the GPD (Great Pasta Disaster) as the local papers★ were to call it. No, that came later . . . and that was much, **MUCH** bigger.

The pasta had been tipped from a huge pan by a very angry man in the upstairs kitchen (which is even more upstairs than the tables at Upstairs at Ample Saki's).

The man was Farflung Heaps and, being the self-appointed leader of the local angry mob, he is very good at being very angry. He shouldn't have been in the kitchen, of course, but he'd STORMED in there to complain. He had been served floppy lettuce and, as far as Farflung Heaps is concerned – and he was VERY concerned – lettuce should be nice and CRISP.

★*The Grubtown Daily Herald* and

The Grubtown Weekly Gerald

At first he'd called over the waitress. She was a very nice girl called Jilly Cheeter who not only used to have the very important job of being Grubtown's official duck-gatherer (bringing all the town's ducks into The Duck House at night)  but – along with her very good friend Mango Claptrap – has been given more medals by Mayor Flabby Gomez than anyone else, except for Mayor Flabby Gomez himself.

Jilly Cheeter is one of those girls just about everyone gets on with apart from Marley Gripe (because he doesn't like children much), Wide

Brim Petty-Mandrake (because he doesn't get on with ANYONE) and the Fox family – Derek and Bunty and their children Shaun, Mantle, Fastbuck and Garrideb – (because they HATE ducks and, as duck-gatherer, it was Jilly's job to be particularly *kind* to ducks).

'This lettuce is floppy!' said Farflung Heaps, picking up a leaf off the top of his side-salad and waving it in Jilly's face. 'Floppy! Floppy! Floppy!'

'I'm – er – sorry, Mr Heaps,' said Jilly Cheeter. 'How should it be?'

'HOW SHOULD IT BE?' shouted Farflung Heaps loud enough to make the woodworm in the walls shake in their little wood-chomped holes, and the rising damp turn round and head back down again. 'HOW SHOULD IT BE?'

The other people in the restaurant did their very best to pretend not to be there.

Farflung Heaps was *glaring* at Jilly Cheeter now. 'THIS LETTUCE SHOULD BE *FRESH*. THAT'S HOW IT SHOULD BE!' he shouted. 'I DEMAND TO SEE THE MANAGER!'

Jilly Cheeter hurried off to find Ample Saki, only to discover that he'd nipped out to count his chickens before they were hatched. She ran to the kitchen and was telling the chef about the floppy lettuce complaint when Heaps himself strode in. He had a flaming torch in one hand and a pitchfork in the other. (He usually carries them about with him, just in case he needs to join an angry mob.)

'Here,' he said to Jilly Cheeter, thrusting the flaming torch into her hand. 'Hold this.'

Before anyone could do anything to stop him, he'd put down his pitchfork, grabbed the giant cooking pot of pasta and tipped its contents out of the window.

'LET THAT BE A LESSON TO YOU ALL!' he shouted. 'DON'T GO THINKING YOU CAN SERVE ME UP FLOPPY LETTUCE AND GET AWAY WITH IT.' He snatched the flaming torch back from Jilly Cheeter just as the smoke detectors detected the smoke coming from it, and the fire sprinklers automatically came on, soaking everyone in Upstairs at Ample Saki's, and downstairs too.

Chapter Two
Crunch Time

There was a picture of Mrs Awning, still tangled in pasta, on the front page of the late editions of that day's *Grubtown Daily Herald*.

The newspaper headline to go with it read:

GRUBTOWN RESIDENT INJURED
BY FALLING PASTA

It didn't mention Mrs Awning by name because she's always having accidents so it wasn't really such exciting news as it would

have been if it had happened to anyone else.

Under the heading was a smaller heading (either called 'a sub-head' or 'Eric', or 'Eric the sub-head', I can't remember which). This read:

LEADER OF ANGRY MOB
SAID TO BE TO BLAME

'Said to be to blame' is a newspaper's way of blaming somebody without actually *admitting* that it's blaming somebody. That way, the person (not) being blamed can't take the newspaper to court and demand BIG MONEY for it blaming them for something they didn't do.

And the article? It began:

Diners at Upstairs at Ample Saki's had their meals disrupted this lunchtime when a row about so-called floppy lettuce apparently led to wqod ewfdhsvbs d svSID HVsd sdvdh SVSRT240 R24R93 2&&e+w+ $%%^sHAPI AEXixjnccncnnccn[Djfd@££44 Kj@9vnvn@

and then went on like that for another twenty lines. The reason? One of the people who works at *The Grubtown Daily Herald* is Hunka Munka who, in his spare time, is a member of the angry mob. It's his job to place the stories the journalists have written in the correct part of the layout. As he was putting this particular article in place, he read it . . .

. . . and it made him VERY ANGRY. How dare Ample Saki give his beloved leader soggy lettuce in his side-salad?!? In fact, Hunka Munka got SO angry that he **PUNCHED** the keyboard, which messed up most of the newspaper story and is why it ended up looking the way it did.

Jilly Cheeter saw the story in the paper and showed it to Mango who was, as always, wearing his ridiculously short shorts.

'Wow,' said Mango Claptrap. 'Mrs Awning does get herself into some tangles. Remember

that time she was bitten by a panda when she opened the wrong box at a charity raffle, and was later hit by the ambulance door when it arrived to take her to hospital?'

Jilly Cheeter was about to reply when Officer Mustard Tripwire came up to them.

'The chief wants to ask you some more questions about what happened at the restaurant the other day, Jilly,' he said.

'Okay,' said Jilly. 'Now?'

'If you don't mind,' said Mustard Tripwire. 'We'll do it down at the station. My police car is just around the corner.'

Mango Claptrap loved the idea of a ride in a police car. 'Can I come too?' he asked.

'Sure you can,' said Tripwire but everything but the 'sure' part was drowned out by a terrible CRUNCHING noise.

All three dashed around

the corner, to find out what was going on. They saw Mayor Flabby Gomez climbing out of his official mayoral car. The official mayoral car is enormous – it has to be to fit Flabby Gomez inside it – and had run over Officer Mustard Tripwire's police vehicle.

'Sorry about that, Tripwire,' said Mayor

Gomez. 'Funny place to park a police car.'

'Sorry, Mister Mayor,' said Officer Tripwire, even though he really knew that the **POLICE VEHICLES ONLY** parking space had been a perfectly *sensible* place to park a police car, and that the accident must have been entirely Flabby Gomez's fault. (You see, the mayor is the most important person in Grubtown, not least because he actually OWNS it, so it's best not to upset him.)

'I was looking for your chief,' said Flabby Gomez, meaning our chief of police, Grabby Hanson.

'I think you'll find him down at the police station, Mister Mayor,' said Officer Tripwire.

'Oh good!' said Flabby Gomez. 'Do you need to get back to the station? If so, I can give you a ride, seeing as how your car looks a little . . .' The mayor paused to look at the tangled

wreck . . . '*flat*,' he said.

'Thanks, Mister Mayor,' said Mustard Tripwire. 'Can Cheeter and Claptrap come too?'

'Sure,' said Flabby. 'Jump in.'

Jilly Cheeter pulled open one of the back doors. A stream of walnuts poured out on to the road.

Chapter Three
Down at the Station

Mustard Tripwire was dying to ask Flabby Gomez why the back of his car was full of walnuts, but thought it best not to say anything.

'Why is the back of your car full of walnuts, Mister Mayor?' asked Mango Claptrap. He and Jilly Cheeter were busy picking up the escaped nuts and putting them back in the car.

'I have absolutely no idea,' said Mayor Gomez. 'I found my swimming pool full of them too. And my briefcase. That's what I want to see the chief about. Let's go!'

Jilly and Mango squeezed in amongst the walnuts. Mango Claptrap had been excited at the idea of being driven around by the mayor in the official mayoral car. But sharing the experience with the walnuts made the whole thing far too *lumpy*.

By the time they'd reached the police station, both he and Jilly Cheeter felt like they'd been massaged by someone with very big and extra-knobbly knuckles. Officer Tripwire had been riding up front with the mayor in the walnut-free part of the car. His journey had been uncomfortable in a very different way: he'd been worrying about what to say to his uncle, Constable Gelatine, about his police car being flattened.

When they arrived at the police station, the mayor disappeared into Chief Grabby Hanson's office with the boarded-up window,

to talk walnuts, and Mustard Tripwire took Jilly and Mango to see Constable Gelatine.

'Ah, thank you for coming in, Miss Cheeter,' he said. Then the police sergeant – Constable is Constable Gelatine's first name, not his police rank – saw the expression on his nephew Mustard's face and let out a long, sad sigh (like the kind of sigh a sad, overweight seal might make when it was thinking of a fish supper but was too lazy to catch any fish). 'What's wrong, Tripwire?' he asked.

'It's the car, uncle – er – *sergeant*,' said Mustard Tripwire. Constable Gelatine didn't like Tripwire calling him 'uncle' unless they were both off-duty.

'What about the car?' asked Sergeant Constable Gelatine.

'It's been flattened. Run over.'

Gelatine immediately thought of Mickey

'Steamroller' Johnson who once ran over **Minty's Cake Shop** and then tried to run over Minty Glibb herself with his steamroller. He'd have been Gelatine's Number One Suspect if it weren't for the fact that he was in jail. 'What happened?' he demanded.

'It was the mayor,' said Officer Tripwire.

'He ran it over in his official car,' said Jilly Cheeter.

'Full of walnuts.'

'Just the back seats,' said Tripwire. (It's important to be accurate when you're a police officer.) 'There were no walnuts up front.'

'The mayor ran over your police vehicle with his official mayoral vehicle, half-filled with walnuts?'

'That's about it, uncle,' said Tripwire.

'Sergeant,' Gelatine reminded him.

'Sorry,' said the young officer. 'Sergeant.'

'Shouldn't be a problem,' said Constable Gelatine. 'Mayor Gomez can always buy us a new one. He's loaded.'

Mustard Tripwire suddenly felt a whole lot happier.

'But being our only police car, that does make things a little awkward,' Gelatine added.

Tripwire felt guilty again.

Constable Gelatine wasn't counting Chief of Police Grabby Hanson's car or their battered old police van. The chief's car is pretty much for the chief's use only, and the police van was on loan to the Grumbly girls. The Grumbly girls are the seven Grumbly daughters – of Mr and Mrs Grumbly – who LOVE to sing songs they've written themselves. I wouldn't say that their songs are really badly written and that they're terrible singers – okay, I just did – but I will say that when the Grumbly girls asked

Chief Grabby Hanson if they could borrow the
van to go to a weekend singing competition
over in Limp, he said 'Yes!' and had given them
the keys and got them out of the door before
you could say, '*Phew! That should get them and
their dreadful voices out of town for a couple of days!*'

So Mustard Tripwire went off to file his
accident report and Constable Gelatine went

through Jilly Cheeter's witness statement regarding Farflung Heaps, Mrs Awning and the pasta. Mango Claptrap, meanwhile, fiddled with the hot-drinks machine in the corridor. By the time he and Jilly Cheeter left, it gave out slerch if you pressed the **TEA** button; tea if you pressed the **SLERCH** button and minestrone soup if you pressed the **COFFEE** button (which was strange because there wasn't even a **MINESTRONE SOUP** button in the first place).

'You shouldn't have done that,' said Jilly Cheeter when Mango Claptrap told her as they were leaving the police station.

'It was an accident,' said Mango. 'You know I love pressing –'

He was about to say 'buttons' but got a mouthful of pasta instead. It was flying through the air EVERYWHERE!

Chapter Four
CRUMPH!

If the window of Chief Grabby Hanson's office hadn't been boarded up, he'd have seen the pasta flying around outside. As it was, it was the loud CRUMPH! which made him leap up from behind his desk, squeeeeeeeeeeeeeeeeeze past Flabby Gomez – no easy thing to do in such a small corner office – and dash past the front counter, down the steps and out into the street, just in time for a second wave, a second downpour of tagliatelle and tomato sauce to

fill the sky.

The pasta came to rest on rooftops, trees, hedges, lamp posts, road-signs, fire hydrants, ducks – LOTS of ducks – cars, roads, pavements and, of course, the citizens of Grubtown themselves. Most of those unlucky enough to have been outside when the blasts of pasta struck – the first mysteriously silent, the second following the CRUMPH – were either covered or badly splattered with pasta and sauce. Even Grabby Hanson had made it outside in

time to have ribbons of pasta land on his peaked chief-of-police cap. Much to his amazement, Mayor Gomez, who'd followed the chief out of the building, not only had tagliatelle land on his head, but a bowl too! Jilly Cheeter and Mango Claptrap, meanwhile, were dripping with the stuff.

Across Grubtown, everyone had their own story to tell about what happened to them the day the pasta struck.

Office-worker Limbo Goulash had been making a phone call from the phone booth outside **The Old Fish Market** (where they sell old fish) when the pasta fell. It was piled so high up against the door that he was trapped for hours …

Over on the illegal gambling ship, *The Crooked Sixpence*, moored just out to sea, the town printer Paltry Feedback had been sitting

on deck with Carlo Monte the riverboat gambler when a huge glumph of pasta knocked him overboard . . .

Purple Outing, owner of **PURPLE OUTING'S MUSIC SHACK** had been unloading CDs and vinyl records outside his shop. When the pasta fell, one CD went flying through the air and straight into Mrs Awning's mouth, where she caught it between her teeth! She slipped, shooting up into the air and coming to land on Marley Gripe who was skidding all over the place on his pasta-covered bike . . .

And me? I had the stuff stuck in my beard for days. (It didn't taste bad.) . . .

As for Jilly Cheeter and Mango Claptrap, they did the kind of thing that has earned them so many medals. Rather than running for cover in case there was a third blast of pasta, or just standing there going, '*I wonder what happened?*', they started running in the direction of where the blasts had come from, keeping their eyes on the ground so as to try to dodge the most slippery splodges.

In the same way that snow can change a familiar landscape into something totally new, the pasta-covered Grubtown took on a whole new look. Unlike somewhere wrapped in a magical white blanket of snow, however, pasta-dripping Grubtown looked plain awful. Imagine walking into a room after a food fight where you haven't had the fun of throwing the

food yourself but are still expected to clear up afterwards . . . now multiply it to the size of a seaside town.

Jilly Cheeter and Mango Claptrap dashed past Slackjaw Gumshoe's Paint and Hardware Store, its exciting pyramid-of-paint-pots window display obscured by plate glass smeared with sauce, ribbons of pasta slowly sliding down it to the pavement below. They saw swarms of delighted seagulls swooping down and tucking into this giant free meal which seemed to have appeared out of nowhere.

One of the stranger sights was that of Wide Brim Petty-Mandrake, our local undertaker, general complainer and least-liked resident of Grubtown, sitting on a three-legged stool outside his house. There wasn't so much as a ribbon of pasta or a speck of sauce on him. He had a spiral-bound notebook open at

the first page and was taking notes. It was obvious he was planning to make a big fuss about what had happened. Petty-Mandrake is always complaining about something. If it's possible, he was even MORE unpopular than usual at that time, because of the trouble and inconvenience he'd caused the town's mobile phone users. (But more on that later.)

At last, Jilly and Mango reached their destination. The two friends hadn't known exactly where the flying pasta had come from, of course, just the general direction but, now they were there, they knew for sure that this was the place.

Himble Street isn't in the best part of town. Most people try to avoid it as much as possible, though I do sometimes go there to buy cheap turnips for the troll who lives in my airing cupboard. (Like most trolls, it loves raw turnips.)

There are quite a few boarded-up shops along there, along with the remains of a candle shop which burnt to the ground. When a water-main burst a few years back, a number of buildings were flooded and some never got pumped-out properly. These became popular haunts for the cooler (more teenagery) ducks to hang out in during the day, along with Mr Carlson who claimed to be a merman but who turned out later just to have webbed feet. Mr Carlson trained as a teacher but, because there are no schools in Grubtown, he became a shampoo-maker when he settled here (before he got taken away).

In amongst this mish-mash of sad buildings is a rather dreary and cheerless ice-cream parlour called CONES, which never seems

to have any customers in it. Next to that is a great big building from which, there was absolutely no doubt whatsoever, the explosions of pasta had come.

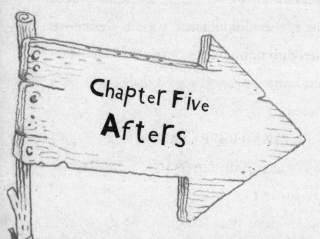

The glass in every single window of **MOLTEN LUSTY'S DISCOUNT CARPET WAREHOUSE** was either broken or missing. The whole building looked like one of those plastic toys you put coloured play dough inside and then press down on to force the dough out through holes to make snake-like shapes. If you think the rest of Grubtown looked pasta-ry, you should have seen this place! **MOLTEN LUSTY'S DISCOUNT CARPET WAREHOUSE** was oozing

pasta and tomato sauce. And there was a great big hole in the roof which the pasta must have exploded through.

There was an enormous banner hanging from the front of the old warehouse which read: **'TA TY PA TA AND CRI PY SAL D AT EXCEL ENT PRI ES'**. (Some of the letters were covered with pasta or sauce.)

Molten Lusty had sold his last discounted carpet long, long ago and the warehouse had been empty for years. Only now someone had obviously been using it to cook up GINORMOUS amounts of pasta. And it didn't take a genius to guess who that someone was.

'FARFLUNG HEAPS!' said Jilly Cheeter and Mango Claptrap together, because there was the leader of the angry mob, who'd got so mad with Jilly at Upstairs at Ample Saki's about the floppy lettuce. He was lying in the arms of

Leggy Johnson (who had been Leggy Prune before she married Mickey 'Steamroller' Johnson in jail). She had dashed out of ⊑◻◻⊑⊑ ice-cream parlour to find out what was going on. It was hard to tell how just badly injured Farflung Heaps was because he was covered in tomato sauce from head to toe so looked very – er – red. He was lying in a very awkward position and it did look like his arms and legs might possibly be bending the wrong way in places. He was also groaning rather a lot.

'Call for an ambulance!' said Leggy Johnson when she saw Jilly and Mango. 'Use the phone in the shop.'

Mango and Jilly dashed inside ⊑◻◻⊑⊑ and behind the counter. Mango lifted the receiver. The phone line was dead. 'There must be pasta on the telephone lines and it's messing things up!' he said.

Of course, any number of us Grubtown citizens own mobile phones, so you'd have thought it would have been easy enough to ask one of us to call for an ambulance  . . . if it wasn't for Wide Brim Petty-Mandrake. Yup, him. He had written SO many letters of complaint to the only mobile phone network covering our town that they had removed their one and only mast just three days previously. Wide Brim Petty-Mandrake wrote the company a total of three-thousand-and-eleven letters and four-hundred-and-twenty e-mails in the space of nine weeks to complain about their mast. Complaints had included ones about the mast's location, height, texture, smell, width, taste – yes, taste – appearance, the

shape of the shadow it cast, and so on and so on and so on. In the end, the Dutch chairwoman of the phone company had piloted her own private helicopter to Grubtown and personally chopped down the mast with an axe she'd brought with her specially. She then left the company and, if the business magazine I read is to be believed, now lives in a cave in the middle of a wood. Without a phone.

So we Grubtowners had to rely on good old-fashioned landline telephones.

Mango and Jilly dashed back out to Leggy Johnson and Farflung Heaps. 'The phone's not working,' said Jilly Cheeter.

'Then we'll have to drive him to the hospital!' said Leggy Johnson.

Now, I'm not a doctor – just an extremely talented (and bearded) author – but I know one thing for sure. If someone is injured and unable

to walk, unless it's absolutely necessary – like they need to get to one of my book-signings, for example – you should leave them where they are. But Leggy Johnson wasn't thinking straight.

'Where's your car?' asked Jilly.

'We'll take him in that,' said Leggy Johnson. She nodded in the direction of a ⌐○⊓⌐⌐ ice-cream van parked outside the parlour.

Jilly and Mango had soon cleared enough pasta and sauce off the ice-cream van's windscreen for Leggy to see out of, and helped her to get Farflung Heaps into the back (using an old door as a stretcher). Mango sat·in the back with the patient, and Jilly sat up-front alongside Mrs Johnson. They were off.

'I wish we had a siren!' Mango Claptrap called from the back.

Jilly Cheeter spotted a big switch on the dashboard and flicked it. Loud music started

blaring out of a speaker mounted on the top of the van, only slightly muffled by ribbons of pasta. 'That should warn people that we're coming!' she shouted. (The distorted music sounded almost as dreadful as one of the Grumbly girls' songs.)

In the back, meanwhile, Mango Claptrap had found that a good way of soothing Farflung Heaps's sore joints was by numbing them with scoops of ice-cream. Chocolate-chip and coffee flavours proved to be particularly good for this. He applied them with a cone.

It wasn't the smoothest of rides because the ice-cream van kept skidding on the fallen pasta, and having to swerve to avoid people, but disaster really struck – within sight of the hospital – when the van hit the pasta-covered Fox family who were lugging a big suitcase in the middle of Trash Street.

Chapter Six
Nuts!

To be more accurate, the ice-cream van hit the enormous suitcase which the (stupid) Foxes had gone and put down in the middle of the road, to have a rest. The suitcase then went flying into Derek, Bunty, Shaun, Mantle, Garrideb and Fastbuck Fox, knocking them down like skittles. It burst open, showering its contents – hundreds of walnuts – everywhere.

Leggy Johnson stayed in the driver's seat, both hands clutching the steering wheel so

tightly that her knuckles were white. Her eyes were as wide open as they could go, and she was rocking herself backwards and forwards, backwards and forwards. Jilly Cheeter jumped out of the van to see if anyone was injured. All six Foxes were already up on their feet and frantically scrabbling around in the pasta to pick up the walnuts and stuff them back in the suitcase.

'Are you okay?' asked Jilly.

'We're fine! Fine!' said Mr Derek Fox.

'Couldn't be better!' said Mrs Bunty Fox.

'N-No harm done,' said Fastbuck Fox, who was limping.

Garrideb Fox said nothing but she gave Jilly a sweet smile, which looked very frightening indeed. Jilly Cheeter had never been smiled at by one of the Fox family before. She'd never had a nice word spoken to her by one of the Fox

family before. As duck-haters they usually hurled abuse or stale buns (or both) at duck-loving Jilly. Yet here they were being perfectly pleasant to her, even though she'd been in a van that had almost run them over. There was something not quite right about this whole thing.

'Look!' said Mango Claptrap, appearing at her side. 'There's Dr Fraud!'

Sure enough, the familiar figure of Dr Fraud, doctor's bag in hand, was hurrying towards them. He'd obviously seen the near miss between the van and the Foxes and wanted to see if he could help. Dr Fraud doesn't work at the hospital. He's not actually a real doctor

but he's an excellent pretend doctor (and much cheaper than the real thing).

Mango Claptrap and Jilly Cheeter led him quickly around to the back of the van to where Farflung Heaps was lying. Dr Fraud gave the injured man a quick examination. 'We need to get him to hospital,' he said at last.

'That's what we were trying to do,' sighed Mango.

Next, Dr Fraud took a look at Leggy Johnson. She was still sitting in the driver's seat. Both hands still clutched the steering wheel so tightly that her knuckles were still white. Her eyes were still as wide open as they could go, and

she was still rocking herself backwards and forwards, backwards and forwards.

'She's suffering from shock,' said Dr Fraud. 'Help me move her over, and I can drive us the last bit of the way to the hospital.'

It turned out that they couldn't get her hands off the wheel, so the pretend doctor used her arms to steer.

And that's how Jilly Cheeter and Mango Claptrap came to be in a makeshift ice-cream ambulance taking the man who was at least partly responsible for the Great Pasta Disaster to Grubtown Hospital, and how they solved the riddle of who'd been filling the mayor's swimming pool, briefcase, official mayoral car and – it later turned out – beach hut and favourite hat with walnuts.

The banner which hung from MOLTEN LUSTY'S DISCOUNT CARPET WAREHOUSE

and read: '**TA TY PA TA AND CRI PY SAL D AT EXCEL ENT PRI ES**' actually said: '**TASTY PASTA AND CRISPY SALAD AT EXCELLENT PRICES**' when the bits of pasta and tomato sauce were wiped away. It turned out that Farflung Heaps had been so ENRAGED – which means really, really, really *angry* – about being served floppy lettuce at Upstairs at Ample Saki's that he'd decided to open up his own pasta-and-CRISPY-salad place to try to win some of Saki's customers. He'd been planning a huge pre-opening party for all the members of his angry mob (plus members of angry mobs from the village of Scrutt and the nearby town of Limp). He'd chosen **MOLTEN LUSTY'S DISCOUNT CARPET WAREHOUSE** because it was (1) cheap to rent; and (2) big enough to fit all those angry people. What he didn't know – well, only Acrid Scorn

knew — was that someone had been storing hazardous (and highly explosive) waste in the old warehouse, which had caught light from a spark from the giant barbecue Farflung Heaps was cooking his pasta and gallons and gallons of tomato sauce on. Acrid Scorn is officially in charge of getting rid of Grubtown's hazardous waste and gets paid quite a lot to do it. As this and other events in the past prove, though, he does have a nasty habit of dumping (or hiding) the stuff locally and pretending to have got rid of it properly. Chief Grabby Hanson is an excellent policeman, but he didn't need to be to work out who'd ditched the waste in the warehouse.

As for the walnuts, Jilly Cheeter and Mango Claptrap were quick to tell the chief about seeing the Foxes with a suitcase full of them, and the chief was quick to tell Mayor Flabby Gomez. If you think Jilly and Mango were

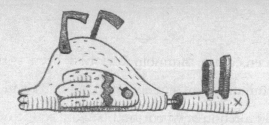

being sneaks/snitches/grasses/informers, you obviously haven't read any other **GRuBtoWN taLes** yet. If you had, you'd know full well that the Foxes – who own a shop called ⚆⚆⚆⚆ ⚆⚆⚆⚆⚆ – deserve all the trouble that comes their way.

And why were they filling Flabby Gomez's life with nuts? The clue, it turned out, lies in a dictionary definition of the word:

nut: [noun] [i] a fruit consisting of a hard shell around an edible kernel. [ii] a nutter or one who is nuts [mad]

Apparently, the Foxes had written to Grubtown Council demanding that a statue

be erected in Brambly Park of a duck with its head stuck in a Wellington boot. The statue had already been carved by Mantle Fox, and a plinth bought for it. The Foxes had even offered to pay to have the whole thing put up. They simply needed the council's permission. When this had been denied, the Foxes approached the mayor directly. When he heard about them wanting to put up a statue of a duck with its head stuck in a Wellington boot, he called

them to his office and told them personally that they must be mad to think that he would ever let this happen. They must be out of their minds. Bonkers. *Nuts* . . .

And that one simple word had led to one of the Fox family's odd-as-always get-your-own-back campaigns.

After a short conversation between Flabby Gomez and Grabby Hanson, it was agreed that the Foxes wouldn't be thrown in jail or fined for their extraordinary behaviour. Judge Mossy Edging gave them 'community service' which, in this instance, meant that they had to clean up the pasta and tomato sauce. All of it. They were lucky that they had the seagulls and Grubtown rats to help them as unpaid volunteers.

Farflung Heaps made a full recovery, except that he can't hear quite as well as he could

before the explosion. Now he shouts even LOUDER when he's angry because, to him, he's only shouting as loudly as he shouted before he went a bit deaf. He's also gone off pasta and doesn't care how floppy his lettuce is.

The one real casualty of this whole messy affair is Leggy Johnson. She sits in her home, still clutching the steering wheel – which they had to unbolt from the CONES ice-cream van – her knuckles white, eyes wide open and rocking backwards and forwards, muttering about walnuts. There's talk about releasing her husband, Mickey 'Steamroller' Johnson, from jail early so that he can look after her.

As for Jilly Cheeter and Mango Claptrap. You guessed it: MORE medals from Flabby Gomez

and their pictures in the papers alongside full details and eye-witness accounts of the Great Pasta Disaster.

THE END

But read on . . .

Another word from Beardy Ardagh

Some people collect bottle tops. Other people collect tummy-button fluff. Some people like sending me letters. These are all useless pastimes but if you **INSIST** on writing to me, be sure to address the envelope:

Beardy Ardagh,
c/o Faber & Faber,
Bloomsbury House
74-77 Great Russell Street
London
WC1B 3DA

and write **GRuBtoWN taLes** in the bottom left-hand corner.

If you're hoping for a reply, DON'T FORGET TO INCLUDE A SELF-ADDRESSED ENVELOPE. (If I had to buy all the stamps and envelopes myself, I'd probably end up having to wear the same vest for a month, and that might frighten my neighbours.) Not that I can promise you'll get a reply, of course. I may peel off the stamp and try selling it back to the Post Office.

Important
instructions from
Beardy Ardagh

Once you've read **The Great Pasta Disaster**, you can flip this book over to see the cover of Kaye Umansky's story. . . then flip it STRAIGHT back again to re-read this **GRuBtoWN taLe**. I don't want to get reports that you've been reading that other story. Anyone would think this is a free country.

And, oh yes, if you haven't done so already, please rush out and buy the first four **GRuBtoWN taLes**. You can find out more about them on the inside front cover.

(Hopefully, you'll also find them in your local or school library, unless some brainless smart Alec has burnt all the books, stuffed the place full of computers and renamed it a 'resource centre'.)

Beardy Ardagh.

Grubtown